ONE DAY
IN THE
LIFE OF
IVAN
DENISOVICH

TRANSLATED FROM THE RUSSIAN BY RALPH PARKER

WITH AN INTRODUCTION BY MARVIN L. KALB

AND A FOREWORD BY ALEXANDER TVARDOVSKY

One Day
in the
Life of
Ivan
Denisovich

BY ALEXANDER SOLZHENITSYN

TIME Reading Program Special Edition

Time-Life Books Inc., Alexandria, Virginia

Time-Life Books Inc.
is a wholly owned subsidiary of
TIME INCORPORATED

TIME Reading Program: *Editor,* Max Gissen

First published in the Soviet Union, 1962.
English translation copyright © 1963 by E. P. Dutton & Co., Inc., New York,
and Victor Gollancz, Ltd., London.
Reprinted 1981.

Library of Congress CIP data following page 178.

For information about any Time-Life book, please write:
Reader Information, Time-Life Books,
541 North Fairbanks Court, Chicago, Illinois 60611

Editors' Preface

Novels written in the Soviet Union have always had a reputation, usually well deserved, for being peculiarly heavy-handed. For years, most Soviet fiction has been written under the oppressive tutelage of political taskmasters wedded to "socialist realism." This doctrine holds that literature, like other forms of art, has only one reason for being: to advance the cause of Communism. The result, with few exceptions, has been a monumentally dull school of fiction that is incapable of persuading the most receptive reader. Perhaps the first point to emphasize about *One Day in the Life of Ivan Denisovich* is that it is not even slightly representative of the breed. Notably lacking in socialist realism, it is one of the most realistic works of fiction ever to emerge from the U.S.S.R.

It is not, of course, a work of art on the scale of Boris Pasternak's masterpiece, *Dr. Zhivago,* another Soviet novel to win a major audience in the United States. *One Day* has, indeed, a curious artlessness about it; not only the dialogue in the book, but also the author's exposition is written in a roughhewn, vernacular prose, quite unlike anything that American readers are accustomed to in Soviet novels. The result is, nevertheless, a story that is immensely readable, and a novel that is manifestly a literary event of importance.

One Day in the Life of Ivan Denisovich was, and remains, a political event. Its original publication, in November of 1962, was patently permitted by Russian leaders because the book seemed useful as an instrument of Soviet policy, which was directed at portraying the Stalin era in the worst possible light. But to readers outside Russia it also afforded remarkable insights into the problems facing the Khrushchev regime.

The story seems a simple one. It begins and ends, as the title suggests, on a single day in the life of a Soviet citizen named Ivan Denisovich Shukov. He is, we learn immediately, a prisoner in a forced-labor camp in Siberia. His problem on the day we are reading about is an elemental one: it is, simply, to get through the day. This will apparently not be very easy, for he awakens feeling sick and feverish, and the temperature outside is 17° below zero. There is, furthermore, a dreadful possibility that his squad will be assigned to work at the new Socialist Way of Life settlement. This would mean a frightful exposure to the elements. "It lay in open country covered with snowdrifts, and before anything else could be done there they would have to dig holes and put up posts and attach barbed wire to them. Wire themselves in, so that they wouldn't run away.

Only then would they start building. There wouldn't be a warm corner for a whole month."

Fortunately, Shukov's squad escapes this assignment and gets another, where there is at least some shelter. This is not entirely a matter of good luck. The preferred assignment is arranged by Tiurin, the squad leader, who bribes a camp official with a pound of salt pork. Tiurin is a veteran of two decades in the labor camps and he knows his way around. Having a knowledgeable squad leader is of tremendous importance, for he is the closest thing to a protector that any of the men have in the camp. Whenever one of them gets a food package from home, some part of it goes to the leader, so that he will have something to bargain with when the need arises.

The salt pork transaction aptly summarizes the morality prevailing in the camp. Among the men themselves, scarcely any favors are done except for a price. And in their dealings with the authorities, the men know that they will be systematically, thoroughly and endlessly cheated. Their bread is short-weighted, their stew is watered, their food packages looted, their extra boots taken from them, and their Sundays, when they are supposed to rest, taken up with senseless make-work projects. When the temperature falls to 41° below zero, the men are not supposed to work outdoors, but they are cheated out of even this pitiful concession to decency: the public thermometer is partially sheltered "so that the registered temperature shouldn't drop too low." Even in their work the men are cheated. Shukov himself is a skilled mason who would take pride in doing a good job, but he is largely thwarted by the inane rules and hopeless conditions under which the jobs have to be performed.

In the end, Shukov does manage to survive the day, physically and spiritually, and in that respect the novel has a happy ending. But reading Alexander Solzhenitsyn's portrait of life in the labor camps must have been a bruising experience for many Soviet men and women. The camps were doubtless better than the Nazi concentration camps and extermination centers; the prevailing spirit among the authorities was not one of sadism, but of simple indifference to the welfare of the prisoners. On the other hand, the camps seem to have been quite a lot worse than those run by the Czar and memorialized by Fëdor Dostoevski in *Memoirs from the House of the Dead*.

To understand the impact this book had, both in the Soviet Union and abroad, it is important to recall several facts about these forced-labor camps. They were, to begin with, a massive operation whose existence, though never mentioned publicly, was well known and anxiously contemplated by Soviet citizens. In the early 1930s, Stalin shipped hundreds of thousands, perhaps millions, of people to the camps for resisting agricultural collectivization. The great purges of 1936 to 1938 sent millions more there, and so did the wartime liquidations of several national minorities. By 1951, during the period described in this book, the total population of the forced-labor camps was probably around

10 million. It has been estimated that around this time they contained no fewer than one sixth of all Soviet adult males.

An operation of these dimensions could not, obviously, be kept secret from the outside world, and the existence of the camps was in fact known to serious students of Soviet affairs for many years. But the camps' existence was not acknowledged by the Soviet government, and it went to the most extraordinary lengths to conceal them from the world; indeed, the development of the Iron Curtain itself, the exclusion of large areas of the nation to travelers, and the overriding habits of secrecy and concealment that have characterized so much of Soviet behavior—and that often seemed so incomprehensible to foreigners—all these were significantly related to the existence of the camps. And, incredible as the fact appears in retrospect, the Soviet government had some success with its denials: millions of well-intentioned and otherwise well-informed adults in the Western democracies accepted the Communist line on the labor camps.

All this has changed. Ever since Nikita Khrushchev began his campaign against Stalin with his 1956 "secret speech," the existence of the camps has been more or less formally acknowledged by the Soviet government. They are still in existence, though on a much smaller scale and populated mostly by criminals and the more dangerous of the "oppositionists"; the paranoia that prevailed in Stalin's day, and that led to wholesale deportations of Soviet citizens who were essentially loyal, is gone.

As NBC chief diplomatic correspondent Marvin Kalb suggests in his Introduction, this novel could not have been published under Khrushchev if it had not happened to fit in with the party policy. In November 1962, when *One Day* first appeared in the literary magazine *Novy Mir*, Krushchev was playing a complex and ambiguous game. He was attempting to keep the still-powerful Stalinists from staging a comeback; *One Day* was obviously suitable ammunition in this campaign, for its rendering of Stalinist injustice and brutality is a powerful one. At the same time, Khrushchev was attempting to maintain the party's rigid control over the ideas of Soviet intellectuals. In a major policy speech in March 1963, he reasserted the primacy of "socialist realism" and again assailed intellectuals who carried their anti-Stalinism too far—who used it as a cloak for anti-Communism.

Altogether, the regime's position involved it in certain large contradictions. For Stalin's outrages were possible only *because* of the party's rigid controls, and every exposure of Stalin strengthened the case for granting more freedoms—freedoms that, it is manifest, Khrushchev had no intention of granting. And so a novel like this presented him with problems too. Soviet intellectuals, given a whiff of freedom, came close to defying the regime when it subsequently insisted on their conformity. One leader of these "liberals," *Novy Mir* editor Alexander Tvardovsky, who first published the novel and whose own foreword to it appears on page xxii, was himself to fall into disfavor.

But if a book like this presents the post-Stalin regime with some problems, it must be noted that they are minimized. The prisoners we meet and sympathize with are essentially loyal to the regime, willing enough to serve it if Stalin's paranoia had not put them in prison. The "crimes" for which the men have been sentenced are not specified in most cases. The reader is not introduced to any real oppositionists; no social democrats, say, or Ukrainian nationalists engage his sympathies. This fact suggests that Solzhenitsyn probably had a pretty good idea of just how far he could go in writing the novel; alternatively it raises a question whether his manuscript might have been edited to eliminate sympathetic portrayals of men whose beliefs are still beyond the pale. Solzhenitsyn himself, then a high-school teacher in Ryazan, remained totally unavailable to the Western press for months after the book appeared.

Despite all the large political issues that have enveloped this book, it is a fine novel, and virtually all serious reviews have identified it as such. It has been available in two different translations. The editors have selected the official translation by Ralph Parker, in preference to another one by Max Hayward and Ronald Hingley. The selection was based primarily on the belief that the Parker translation more faithfully renders the Russian original and more plausibly captures the author's intentions. In addition, the official version seemed preferable precisely *because* this book was a political event. Part of the worldwide interest in the novel resides in the very fact that it was passed by Soviet censors and published in the U.S.S.R. To see what the Russians were allowed to read in the days of the thaw, it seemed best to get the official version.

—THE EDITORS

Introduction

On November 20, 1962, *Novy Mir,* a monthly Soviet literary magazine, published a short novel by an unknown Russian writer, Alexander Isayevich Solzhenitsyn, entitled *One Day in the Life of Ivan Denisovich.* It was an immediate literary and political sensation. Within a day all of the ninety-five thousand copies of the November issue of the magazine were snapped up by eager Russians. Within a week Solzhenitsyn skyrocketed to international fame from an obscure job teaching mathematics in Ryazan, a small provincial town not too far from Moscow; and his title character, Ivan Denisovich Shukhov, was quickly recognized throughout the country as a touching symbol of the suffering which the Russian people had endured under the Stalinist system.

Was there anything special about Ivan that sparked this lightning response? Not really. Ivan was an ordinary Russian caught up in the swirl and chaos of World War II. Like millions of other Russians, he served uncomplainingly in the Red Army for four years, surviving.the bitter cold and hunger of the Western front. In 1945, he and a friend were captured by the Germans. After a few days they managed to escape and returned to Russian lines. Ironically, instead of being decorated for heroism and loyalty, Ivan was arrested by Stalin's supersensitive secret police, who accused him of high treason and charged that he had returned only to spy for the Germans. Confused and helpless, afraid that he would be shot if he tried to explain, Ivan "confessed." He was sentenced to ten years in a Siberian concentration camp. Solzhenitsyn's book describes one day in that camp, one day no better and no worse than any of the other three thousand six hundred and fifty-two days of Ivan's sentence. Ivan's experience was no isolated miscarriage of justice; it was typical of the Stalinist system, under which the labor camps of Siberia were crowded with Russians whose "crime" may have been nothing greater than a careless remark about Stalin to a tattletale neighbor. There was hardly a Russian family that managed to escape this tragic fate. Almost every one of them had a father or a husband or a son or a cousin who "sat"— the Russian euphemism for serving a term, generally unwarranted, in the camps. That is why *One Day,* the first book about this black page of the Stalin era ever to appear in the Soviet Union, had such a profound impact on the Russian people. By its brevity and simple power, it forced a Russian reader to remember the days of Stalin.

Many Russians do not want to remember: the victims of Stalinist injustice find it too painful; and the accomplices find it too shattering—especially now, after several years of relative normalcy. But there are others who want Russia to remember. Although Solzhenitsyn is undoubtedly a writer with bold views, it is important to note that his novel was published because it suited Khrushchev's domestic policy at that time. Its unstated but obvious message—the devastating impact of Stalinism on ordinary Russians—fit neatly into the pattern of Khrushchev's continuing attack against Stalin's abuses.

When Solzhenitsyn finished his book, the manuscript was sent to several magazines and was rejected by all of them; apparently the editors found its theme too explosive to handle on their own authority. At last, the manuscript fell into the hands of the "liberal wing" of the Soviet literary world, represented by such writers as, among others, Alexander Tvardovsky, editor of *Novy Mir*.

They felt strongly that *One Day* should be published, but they too were unable to make such a decision on their own. They turned to the Central Committee of the Communist Party for a decision. The members of the Central Committee debated the merits of publication; they were sharply divided. The final decision, as usual, was made by Premier Khrushchev, who is said to have read the book and personally approved its uncensored publication. In a speech before a major Central Committee meeting which took place the week the book came out, Khrushchev revealed his own role in the decision to publish it. An additional five thousand copies were made available to the top Communists attending the meeting.

At the same time, government publications launched a

coordinated campaign to give the novel maximum publicity: *Soviet Literature* translated it into English; *Moscow News*, a weekly newspaper for foreign consumption, was authorized to run a serialized version; and *Izvestia* and other nonliterary newspapers published highly favorable reviews of the book.

Even without this official encouragement, the book would have been a sensation in Russia—not only because of its sensitive subject but also because of its literary merit. *One Day* represents no literary innovation. Its form and style are conventional, following the nineteenth-century Russian tradition of the "social protest" novel. But it tells a story about little people trapped in a merciless political machine in a way that lifts it high above the level of the average Soviet "man-loves-tractor" school of literature.

Solzhenitsyn's language is direct and powerful, reminding some Russian critics of the young Dostoevsky, who, in his *Notes from Underground,* managed to convey a unique impression of nineteenth-century Russia through the eyes and thoughts of a man holed up in a basement. Using this same effective literary device—seeing and understanding the world through the eyes and mind of the leading character—Solzhenitsyn presents an unadorned and starkly disturbing picture of life in a Russian concentration camp. He traces one day in Ivan's life, from reveille to lights-out. He never intrudes in Ivan's story, and the reader quickly identifies with Ivan the man and Ivan the prisoner.

One chills to the 17°-below-zero cold of Siberia. One

sympathizes with the poor peasant who wants to go home but is afraid even to think about it. One grasps the meaning of Ivan's sad, wise question: "How can you expect a man who's warm to understand a man who's cold?" One understands why Ivan has become indifferent, and cannot even write a letter home. "Writing now was like dropping stones in some deep, bottomless pool. They drop; they sink—but there is no answer." One even understands why Ivan signed a confession saying he had returned to Russian lines "to carry out a mission for German intelligence." And one begins to comprehend the simple, futile, and monotonous horror of the labor-camp system as one reads the last few lines of the book:

"Shukhov went to sleep fully content. He'd had many strokes of luck that day: they hadn't put him in the cells; they hadn't sent his squad to the settlement; he'd swiped a bowl of kasha at dinner; he'd built a wall and enjoyed doing it; he'd smuggled a bit of hacksaw blade through; he'd earned a favor from Tsezar that evening; he'd bought that tobacco. And he hadn't fallen ill. He'd got over it.

"A day without a dark cloud. Almost a happy day.

"There were three thousand six hundred and fifty-three days like that in his stretch. From the first clang of the rail to the last clang of the rail.

"Three thousand six hundred and fifty-three days.

"The three extra days were for leap years."

Solzhenitsyn conveys the power and drama of prison life in a style marked by understatement. His economy of words is not a Slavic quality. Yet Solzhenitsyn is a Slav. He was born in 1918, a year after the Bolsheviks stormed to power throughout Russia. Although his novel draws on his own experiences, it is not strictly autobiographical; for Solzhenitsyn, unlike his simple peasant hero, came from a "petit-bourgeois" family. When he was a boy, his father died; and he was brought up by his mother in the southern city of Rostov. He completed his ten-year school and enrolled at the University of Rostov, where he majored in physics and mathematics.

In 1941, his life, and Russia's, changed drastically. The Germans invaded Russia, and Solzhenitsyn was drafted into the Red Army. In 1942, he took an artillery course and became commander of an artillery battery, where he served with distinction for three years. He was twice decorated for bravery.

In February 1945, he was arrested in East Prussia on what Tass calls a "baseless political charge" and sentenced to eight years' imprisonment. According to one story, Solzhenitsyn was supposed to have made a derogatory remark about Stalin. For the next eight years, he was in a Russian concentration camp, where he survived the experiences he later described in *One Day*. In 1953, after the death of Stalin, he was released from the camp but was still forced to live in exile in Central Asia, where he remained until after Khrushchev's historic "secret speech" denouncing Stalin at the 20th Party Congress in February 1956.

Solzhenitsyn was rehabilitated in 1957 "in the absence of

corpus delicti." He moved to Ryazan, married a chemistry student, and began to teach mathematics at the local ten-year school. In his spare time, he started to write, drawing on his own experiences and observations of people in a small Russian town. *One Day* was his first published work, and it became a popular sensation because its subject was meaningful for every Soviet citizen; it awakened deeply buried memories and touched deep chords of guilt and despair.

It was a literary sensation because of its simple power, its ability to envelop the reader in the futile atmosphere of camp life and to make him see it through the eyes of a Russian peasant who accepts everything, both good and evil, with enduring patience as he has done for centuries under every conceivable kind of misrule.

It was an official sensation because it humanized the cold clichés of Khrushchev's attacks on Stalinist "violations of socialist legality," and made his drive to eliminate these abuses more comprehensive to the average Russian.

But beyond all this, *One Day* raised a major question: how far had Khrushchev stretched the limits of what can and cannot be said in print? Although this was a bold and original book, could it have been bolder if the system had not held it back? There were old Bolsheviks who, while praising *One Day,* pointed out that there was more to the labor-camp story than fatalistic acceptance. The innocent Ivans, unprotesting and mild, were the majority; but there were others, more politically sophisticated, who refused to accept the injustices of the system which had sent them, guiltless, into the labor camps, and who refused to cooperate in any way with the authorities.

Unlike Ivan, they took no simple pride in getting through another day and building a fine wall. They planned and occasionally tried to carry out revolts. They called themselves the Blacks; they called the Ivans the Reds.

Solzhenitsyn wrote nothing about these people, the old Bolsheviks complained. Perhaps Solzhenitsyn did not know them. Perhaps his experience was limited to Ivans. Perhaps he knew of the others but considered them irrelevant to his story of the typical suffering Russian peasant. Or, perhaps, he would have written more, but could not because of the limits of Soviet literary policy at that time.

Solzhenitsyn's more recent personal history—his exile from Russia and subsequent residence in the United States—as well as some of his newer works such as *The Gulag Archipelago* and *The Oak and the Calf* have shown him to be more a champion of his own talent than of the liberalizing of the Soviet literary scene. In fact, if Solzhenitsyn can be said to have a cause, it might be the combined belief in his artistic skill and his use of it to celebrate his private vision of a more pastoral, non-Communist Russia.

Solzhenitsyn has been accused of disloyalty to *Novy Mir* and Tvardovsky, perhaps because he used the magazine as a mouthpiece for his views but gave little assistance to Tvardovsky's avowed cause: freeing Soviet literature from harsh political constraints. In addition, Solzhenitsyn saw no ideological conflict in permitting his work to appear in such rigid and doctrinaire journals as *Oktiabr*. Liberals such as Tvardovsky viewed this as betrayal.

Whatever Solzhenitsyn's methods of getting his work in print, we must be grateful for the publication, against great odds, of *One Day in the Life of Ivan Denisovich,* and for the light it shed on what until then had been one of the darkest corners of the Soviet world.

—MARVIN L. KALB

Foreword to the Original Edition

The raw material of life which serves as a basis for A. Solzhenitsyn's story is unusual in Soviet literature. It carries within itself an echo of the painful features in our development related to the cult of personality that has been debunked and repudiated by the Party, features that, although they are not so far away from us in time, nevertheless seem to us to be in the distant past. But the past, no matter what it was like, never becomes a matter of indifference to the present. The assurance of a complete and irrevocable break with everything which beclouds the past lies in a true and courageous comprehension of its full consequences. It was about this that N. S. Khrushchev spoke in his concluding words at the 22nd Congress of the Communist Party of the Soviet Union, words so memorable for all of us: "It is our duty to gain a thorough and comprehensive understanding of the nature of the matters related to the abuse of power. Time will pass and we shall die, we are all mortal, but so long as we work we can and must clear up many points and tell the truth to the Party and to the people.... This we must do so that such things never happen again."

One Day in the Life of Ivan Denisovich is not a document in the sense of being a memoir, nor is it notes or reminiscences of the author's personal experiences, although only such personal experiences could lend this story its sense of genuine authenticity. This is a work of art and it is by virtue of the artistic interpretation of this material from life that it is a witness of special value, a document of an art which up to now had seemed to have few possibilities.

The reader will not find in A. Solzhenitsyn's story an all-encompassing portrayal of that historic period which is particularly marked by the bitter memory of the year 1937. The content of *One Day* is naturally limited in time and place of action and the horizons of the main hero of the story. But in the writing of A. Solzhenitsyn, who here enters the literary scene for the first time, one day in the life of the camp prisoner, Ivan Denisovich Shukhov, develops into a picture which gives extraordinary vitality and fidelity to the truthfulness of its human characters. Herein above all lies the uncommon power of the work to impress. The reader can visualize for himself many of the people depicted here in the tragic role of camp inmates in other situations—at the front or at postwar construction sites. They are the same people who by the will of circumstance have been put to severe physical and moral tests under special and extreme conditions.

In this story there is no deliberate concentration of terrible facts of the cruelty and arbitrariness that were the result of the violation of Soviet legality. The author chose instead to portray only one of the most ordinary of days in the life at camp from reveille to retreat. Nevertheless this "ordinary" day cannot but arouse in the heart of the reader a bitter feeling of pain for the fate of the people who, from the pages of this story, rise up before us so alive and so near. Yet the unquestionable victory of the artist lies in the fact that the bitterness and the pain have nothing in common with a feeling of hopeless depression. On the contrary, the impression left by this work is so extraordinary in its unvarnished and difficult truth that it somehow frees the soul of the burden of things unsaid that needed to be said and at the same time it strengthens one's manly and lofty feelings.

This is a grim story—still another example of the fact that there are no areas or facts of reality that can be excluded from the sphere of the Soviet artist in our days or that are beyond truthful portrayal. Everything depends on the capabilities of the artist himself.

This story leads to still another simple and instructive conclusion: the truly significant content, the fidelity to the great truths of life, the profound humanity in the approach to the portrayal of even the most difficult subjects cannot but awake corresponding virtues in the author's writing. *One Day* is alive and distinctive in its very everyday ordinariness and outward unassumingness; it is least of all concerned with itself and is therefore full of an inner dignity and force.

I do not want to anticipate the evaluation of this work— not so great in size—although for me it is indubitable that it signifies the entrance into our literature of a new, original, and completely mature artist.

It is possible that the author's use—a quite moderate and advisable use, by the way—of some words and expressions of the environment in which the hero spends his working day will provoke the objections of fastidious taste. But on the whole *One Day in the Life of Ivan Denisovich* belongs with those works of literature which, once we have read them, create in us a deep desire to have our feeling of gratitude to the author shared by other readers too.

—ALEXANDER TVARDOVSKY

One Day
in the
Life of
Ivan
Denisovich

At five o'clock that morning reveille was sounded, as usual, by the blows of a hammer on a length of rail hanging up near the staff quarters. The intermittent sounds barely penetrated the windowpanes on which the frost lay two fingers thick, and they ended almost as soon as they'd begun. It was cold outside, and the campguard was reluctant to go on beating out the reveille for long.

The clanging ceased, but everything outside still looked like the middle of the night when Ivan Denisovich Shukhov got up to go to the bucket. It was pitch dark except for the yellow light cast on the window by three lamps—two in the outer zone, one inside the camp itself.

And no one came to unbolt the barracks door; there was no sound of the barrack orderlies pushing a pole into place to lift the barrel of excrement and carry it out.

Shukhov never overslept reveille. He always got up at once, for the next ninety minutes, until they assembled for work, belonged to him, not to the authorities, and any old-timer could always earn a bit—by sewing a pair of mittens for someone out of old sleeve lining; or bringing some rich loafer in the squad his dry valenki[1]—right up to his bunk, so that he wouldn't have to stumble barefoot round the heap of boots looking for his own pair; or going the rounds of the warehouses, offering to be of service, sweeping up this or fetching that; or going to the mess hall to collect bowls from the tables and bring them stacked to the dishwashers—you're sure to be given something to eat there, though there were plenty of others at that game, more than plenty—and, what's worse, if you found a bowl with something left in it you could hardly resist licking it out. But Shukhov had never forgotten the words of his first squad leader, Kuziomin—a hard-bitten prisoner who had already been in for twelve years by 1943— who told the newcomers, just in from the front, as they sat beside a fire in a desolate cutting in the forest:

"Here, men, we live by the law of the taiga. But even here people manage to live. The ones that don't make it are those who lick other men's leftovers, those who count on the doctors to pull them through, and those who squeal on their buddies."

As for squealers, he was wrong there. Those people were sure to get through camp all right. Only, they were saving their own skin at the expense of other people's blood.

Shukhov always arose at reveille. But this day he didn't. He had felt strange the evening before, feverish, with pains all over his body. He hadn't been able to get warm all through the night. Even in his sleep he had felt at one

[1] Knee-length felt boots for winter wear.

moment that he was getting seriously ill, at another that he was getting better. He had wished morning would never come.

But the morning came as usual.

Anyway, where would you get warm in a place like this, with the windows iced over and the white cobwebs of frost all along the huge barracks where the walls joined the ceiling!

He didn't get up. He lay there in his bunk on the top tier, his head buried in a blanket and a coat, both feet stuffed into one tucked-under sleeve of his wadded jacket.

He couldn't see, but his ears told him everything going on in the barrack room and especially in the corner his squad occupied. He heard the heavy tread of the orderlies carrying one of the big barrels of excrement along the passage outside. A light job, that was considered, a job for the infirm, but just you try and carry out the muck without spilling any. He heard some of the 75th slamming bunches of boots onto the floor from the drying shed. Now their own men were doing it (it was their own squad's turn, too, to dry valenki). Tiurin, the squad leader, and his deputy Pavlo put on their valenki without a word but he heard their bunks creaking. Now Pavlo would be going off to the bread-storage and Tiurin to the staff quarters to see the P.P.D.[1]

Ah, but not simply to report as usual to the authorities for the daily assignment. Shukhov remembered that this morning his fate hung in the balance: they wanted to shift the 104th from the building shops to a new site, the Socialist

[1] Production Planning Department.

Way of Life settlement. It lay in open country covered with snowdrifts, and before anything else could be done there they would have to dig holes and put up posts and attach barbed wire to them. Wire themselves in, so that they wouldn't run away. Only then would they start building.

There wouldn't be a warm corner for a whole month. Not even a doghouse. And fires were out of the question. There was nothing to build them with. Let your work warm you up, that was your only salvation.

No wonder the squad leader looked so worried, that was his job—to elbow some other squad, some bunch of suckers, into the assignment instead of the 104th. Of course with empty hands you got nowhere. He'd have to take a pound of salt pork to the senior official there, if not a couple of pounds.

There's never any harm in trying, so why not have a go at the dispensary and get a few days off if you can? After all, he did feel as though every limb was out of joint.

Then Shukhov wondered which of the campguards was on duty that morning. It was "One-and-a-half" Ivan's turn, he recalled. Ivan was a thin, weedy, dark-eyed sergeant. At first sight he looked like a real bastard, but when you got to know him he turned out to be the most good-natured of the guards on duty: he didn't put you in the guardhouse, he didn't haul you off before the authorities. So Shukhov decided he could lie in his bunk a little longer, at least while Barracks 9 was at the mess hall.

The whole four-bunk frame began to shake and sway. Two of its occupants were getting up at the same time: Shukhov's top-tier neighbor, Alyosha the Baptist, and Buinovsky, the ex-naval captain down below.

The orderlies, after removing both barrels of excrement, began to quarrel about which of them should go for hot water. They quarreled naggingly, like old women.

"Hey you, cackling like a couple of hens!" bellowed the electric welder in the 20th squad. "Get going." He flung a boot at them.

The boot thudded against a post. The squabbling stopped.

In the next squad the deputy squad leader growled quietly: "Vasily Fyodorovich, they've cheated us again at the supply depot, the dirty rats. They should have given us four twenty-five-ounce loaves and I've only got three. Who's going to go short?"

He kept his voice down, but of course everyone in the squad heard him and waited fearfully to learn who would be losing a slice of bread that evening.

Shukhov went on lying on his sawdust mattress, as hard as a board from long wear. If only it could be one thing or the other—let him fall into a real fever or let his aching joints ease up.

Meanwhile Alyosha was murmuring his prayers and Buinovsky had returned from the latrines, announcing to no one in particular but with a sort of malicious glee: "Well, sailors, grit your teeth. It's twenty below, for sure."

Shukhov decided to report sick.

At that very moment his blanket and jacket were imperiously jerked off him. He flung his coat away from his face and sat up. Looking up at him, his head level with the top bunk, was the lean figure of The Tartar.

So the fellow was on duty out of turn and had stolen up.

"S 854," The Tartar read from the white strip that had been stitched to the back of his black jacket. "Three days' penalty with work."

The moment they heard that peculiar choking voice of his, everyone who wasn't up yet in the whole dimly lit barracks, where two hundred men slept in bug-ridden bunks, stirred to life and began dressing in a hurry.

"What for, citizen[1] chief?" asked Shukhov with more chagrin than he felt in his voice.

With work—that wasn't half so bad. They gave you hot food and you had no time to start thinking. Real jail was when you were kept back from work.

"Failing to get up at reveille. Follow me to the camp commandant's office," said The Tartar lazily.

His crumpled, hairless face was imperturbable. He turned, looking around for another victim, but now everybody, in dim corners and under the lights, in upper bunks and in lower, had thrust their legs into their black wadded trousers or, already dressed, had wrapped their coats around themselves and hurried to the door to get out of the way until The Tartar had left.

Had Shukhov been punished for something he deserved he wouldn't have felt so resentful. What hurt him was that he was always one of the first to be up. But he knew he

---

[1] Prisoners were not allowed to use the word comrade.

couldn't plead with The Tartar. And, protesting merely for the sake of form, he hitched up his trousers (a bedraggled scrap of cloth had been sewn on them, just above the left knee, with a faded black number), slipped on his jacket (here the same digits appeared twice—on the chest and on the back), fished his valenki from the heap on the floor, put his hat on (with his number on a patch of cloth at the front), and followed The Tartar out of the barrack room.

The whole 104th saw him go, but no one said a word— what was the use, and anyway what could they say? The squad leader might have tried to do something, but he wasn't there. And Shukhov said nothing to anyone. He didn't want to irritate The Tartar. Anyway he could rely on the others in his squad to keep his breakfast for him.

The two men left the barracks. The cold made Shukhov gasp.

Two powerful searchlights swept the camp from the farthest watchtowers. The border lights, as well as those inside the camp, were on. There were so many of them that they outshone the stars.

With the snow creaking under their boots, the prisoners hurried away, each on his own business, some to the parcels office, some to hand in cereals to be cooked in the "individual" kitchen. All kept their heads down, buried in their buttoned-up coats, and all were chilled to the bone, not so much from the actual cold as from the prospect of having to spend the whole day in it. But The Tartar in his old army coat with the greasy blue tabs walked at a steady pace, as though the cold meant nothing to him.

They walked past the high wooden fence around the guardhouse, the only brick building in the camp; past the barbed wire that protected the camp bakery from the prisoners; past the corner of the staff quarters where the length of frosted rail hung on thick strands of wire; past another pole with a thermometer hanging on it (in a sheltered spot, so that the registered temperature shouldn't drop too low). Shukhov looked hopefully out of the corner of an eye at the milk-white tube—if it had shown −41° they ought not to be sent out to work. But today it was nowhere near −41°.

They walked into the staff quarters and The Tartar led him straight to the guardroom; and Shukhov realized, as he had guessed on the way there, that he wasn't being sent to the guardhouse at all—it was simply that the guardroom floor needed scrubbing. The Tartar told him he was going to let him off, and ordered him to scrub the floor.

Scrubbing the guardroom floor had been the job of a special prisoner who wasn't sent to work outside the camp—a staff orderly. The fellow had long ago made himself at home in the staff quarters; he had access to the offices of the camp commandant, the man in charge of discipline, and the security officer (the Father Confessor, they called him). When working for them he sometimes heard things that even the guards didn't know, and after a time he got a big head and came to consider scrubbing the floor for rank-and-file camp-guards a bit beneath him. Having sent for him once or twice, the guards discovered what was in the wind and began to pick on other prisoners for the floor-scrubbing.

In the guardroom the stove was throwing out a fierce heat. Two guards in grubby tunics were playing checkers, and a third, who had not bothered to remove his sheepskin and valenki, lay snoring on a narrow bench. In one corner of the room stood an empty pail with a rag inside.

Shukhov was delighted. He thanked The Tartar for letting him off and said: "From now on I'll never get up late again."

The rule in this place was a simple one: when you'd finished you left. And now that he'd been given work to do, Shukhov's aches and pains seemed to have gone. He picked up the pail and, bare-handed—in his hurry he'd forgotten to take his mittens from under his pillow—went to the well.

Several of the squad leaders who were on their way to the P.P.D. had gathered near the pole with the thermometer, and one of the younger ones, a former Hero of the Soviet Union, shinnied up it and wiped off the instrument.

The others shouted advice from below:

"See you don't breathe on it. It'll push up the temperature."

"Push it up? Not ——ing likely. *My* breath won't have any effect."

Tiurin of the 104th—Shukhov's squad—was not among them. Shukhov put down the pail, tucked his hands into his sleeves, and watched with interest.

The man up the pole shouted hoarsely: "Seventeen and a half. Not a damn bit more."

And, taking another look to be sure, slid down.

"Oh, it's cockeyed. It always lies," someone said. "Do you think they'd ever hang one up that gave the true temperature?"

The squad leaders scattered. Shukhov ran to the well. The frost was trying to nip his ears under his earflaps, which he had lowered but not tied.

The top of the well was so thickly coated with ice that he only just managed to slip the bucket into the hole. The rope hung stiff as a ramrod.

With numb hands he carried the dripping bucket back to the guardroom and plunged his hands into the water. It felt warm.

The Tartar was no longer there. The guards—there were four now—stood in a group. They'd given up their checkers and their nap and were arguing about how much cereal they were going to get in January (food was in short supply at the settlement, and although rationing had long since come to an end, certain articles were sold to them, at a discount, which were not available to the civilian inhabitants).

"Shut that door, you scum. There's a draft," said one of the guards.

No sense in getting your boots wet in the morning. Even if Shukhov had dashed back to his barracks he wouldn't have found another pair to change into. During eight years' imprisonment he had known various systems for allocating footwear: there'd been times when he'd gone through the winter without valenki at all, or leather boots either, and had had to make shift with rope sandals or a sort of galoshes made of scraps of motor tires—"Chetezes" they called them, after the Cheliabinsk tractor works. Now the footwear situation seemed better; in October Shukhov had received (thanks to Pavlo, whom he trailed to the warehouse) a pair of ordinary, hard-wearing leather boots, big enough for a double thickness of rags inside. For a week he went about as though he'd been given a birthday present, kicking his new heels. Then in December the valenki arrived, and, oh, wasn't life wonderful?

But some devil in the bookkeeper's office had whispered in the commandant's ear that valenki should be issued only to those who surrendered their boots. It was against the rules for a prisoner to possess two pairs of footwear at the same time. So Shukhov had to choose. Either he'd have to wear leather throughout the winter, or surrender the boots and wear valenki even in the thaw. He'd taken such good care of his new boots, softening the leather with grease! Ah, nothing had been so hard to part with in all his eight years in camps as that pair of boots! They were tossed into a common heap. Not a hope of finding your own pair in the spring.

Now Shukhov knew what he had to do. He dexterously pulled his feet out of the valenki, put the valenki in a corner, stuffed his foot rags into them (his spoon tinkled on the floor —though he'd made himself ready for the guardhouse in a hurry, he hadn't forgotten his spoon), and, barefoot, sloshed the water right under the guards' valenki.

"Hey there, you slob, take it easy," one of the guards shouted, putting his feet on a chair.

"Rice?" another went on. "Rice is in a different category. You can't compare cereal with rice."

"How much water are you going to use, idiot? Who on earth washes like that?"

"I'll never get it clean otherwise, citizen chief. It's thick with mud."

"Didn't you ever watch your wife scrub the floor, pig?"

Shukhov drew himself up, the dripping rag in his hand. He smiled ingenuously, revealing the gaps in his teeth, the result of a touch of scurvy at Ust-Izhma in 1943. And what a touch it was—his exhausted stomach wouldn't hold any kind of food, and his bowels could move nothing but a bloody fluid. But now only a lisp remained from that old trouble.

"I was taken away from my wife in forty-one, citizen chief. I've forgotten what she was like."

"That's the way the scum wash. . . . They don't know how to do a ——ing thing and don't want to learn. They're not worth the bread we give them. We ought to feed them on ——."

"Anyway, what's the ——ing sense in washing it every day? Who can stand the damp? Look here, you, 854. Just wipe it over lightly to make it moist and then —— off."

"No, you can't compare cereal with rice."

Shukhov knew how to manage anything.

Work was like a stick. It had two ends. When you worked

for the knowing you gave them quality; when you worked for a fool you simply gave him eyewash.

Otherwise, everybody would have croaked long ago. They all knew that.

Shukhov wiped the floorboards with a damp rag so that no dry patches remained, tossed the rag behind the stove without wringing it out, pulled on his valenki near the door, threw out the rest of the water onto the path used by the camp authorities, and, taking short cuts, made a dash past the bathhouse and the dark, cold club to the mess hall.

He still had to fit in a visit to the dispensary. He ached all over. And there was that guard outside the mess hall to be dodged—the camp commandant had issued strict orders that prisoners on their own were to be picked up and thrown into the guardhouse.

That morning—a stroke of luck—there was no crowd, no lines, outside the mess. Walk in.

The air was as thick as in a Turkish bath. An icy wave blew in through the door and met the steam rising from the stew. The squads sat at tables or crowded the aisles in between, waiting for places to be freed. Shouting to each other through the crush, two or three men from each squad carried bowls of stew and oatmeal on wooden trays and tried to find room for them on the tables. Look at that damn stiff-necked fool. He doesn't hear, he's bumped a tray. Splash, splash! You've a hand free, hit him on the back of the neck. That's the way. Don't stand there blocking the aisle, looking for something to swipe!

There at the table, before dipping his spoon in, a young man crossed himself. A West Ukrainian, that meant, and a new arrival too.

As for the Russians, they'd forgotten which hand to cross themselves with.

They sat in the cold mess hall, most of them eating with their hats on, eating slowly, picking out putrid little fish from under leaves of boiled black cabbage and spitting the bones out on the table. When the bones formed a heap and it was the turn of another squad, someone would sweep them off and they'd be trodden into a mush on the floor. But it was considered bad manners to spit the fishbones straight out on the floor.

Two rows of trestles ran down the middle of the hall and near one of them sat Fetiukov of the 104th. It was he who was keeping Shukhov's breakfast for him. Fetiukov had the last place in his squad, lower than Shukhov's. From the outside, everyone in the squad looked the same—their numbered black coats were identical—but within the squad there were great distinctions. Everyone had his grade. Buinovsky, for instance, was not the sort to sit keeping another zek's[1] bowl for him. And Shukhov wouldn't take on any old job either. There were others lower than him.

Fetiukov caught sight of Shukhov and with a sigh surrendered his place.

"It's all cold. I was just going to eat your helping. Thought you were in the guardhouse."

[1] Abbreviation of Russian for prisoner.

He didn't hang around—no hope for any leftovers to scrape out of Shukhov's bowl.

Shukhov pulled his spoon out of his boot. His little baby. It had been with him his whole time in the North, he'd cast it with his own hands in sand out of aluminum wire, and it was embossed with the words "Ust-Izhma 1944."

Then he removed his hat from his clean-shaven head—however cold it might be, he could never bring himself to eat with his hat on—and stirred the cold stew, taking a quick look to see what kind of helping they'd given him. An average one. They hadn't ladled it from the top of the kettle, but they hadn't ladled it from the bottom either. Fetiukov was the sort who when he was looking after someone else's bowl took the potatoes from it.

The only good thing about stew was that it was hot, but Shukhov's portion had grown quite cold. However, he ate it with his usual slow concentration. No need to hurry, not even for a house on fire. Apart from sleep, the only time a prisoner lives for himself is ten minutes in the morning at breakfast, five minutes over dinner, and five at supper.

The stew was the same every day. Its composition depended on the kind of vegetable provided that winter. Nothing but salted carrots last year, which meant that from September to June the stew was plain carrot. This year it was black cabbage. The most nourishing time of the year was June; then all vegetables came to an end and were replaced by grits. The worst time was July—then they shredded nettles into the pot.

The little fish were more bone than flesh; the flesh had

been boiled off the bone and had disintegrated, leaving a few remnants on head and tail. Without neglecting a single fish scale or particle of flesh on the brittle skeleton, Shukhov went on chomping his teeth and sucking the bones, spitting the remains on the table. He ate everything—the gills, the tail, the eyes when they were still in their sockets but not when they'd been boiled out and floated in the bowl separately— big fish-eyes. Not then. The others laughed at him for that.

This morning Shukhov economized. Since he hadn't returned to the barracks he hadn't drawn his rations, so he ate his breakfast without bread. He'd eat the bread later. Might be even better that way.

After the vegetable stew there was *magara,* that damned "Chinese" oatmeal. It had grown cold too, and had set into a solid lump. Shukhov broke it up into pieces. It wasn't only that the oatmeal was cold—it was tasteless even when hot, and left you no sense of having filled your belly. Just grass, except that it was yellow, and looked like cereal. They'd got the idea of serving it instead of cereals from the Chinese, it was said. When boiled, a bowlful of it weighed nearly a pound. Not much of an oatmeal but that was what it passed for.

Licking his spoon and tucking it back into his boot, Shukhov put on his hat and went to the dispensary.

The sky was still quite dark. The camp lights drove away the stars. The broad beams of the two searchlights were still sweeping the zone. When this camp, this "special" (forced-labor) camp, had been organized, the security forces had a lot of flares left over from the war, and whenever there was a power failure they shot up flares over the zone—white, green, and red—just like real war. Later they stopped using them. To save money, maybe.

It seemed just as dark as at reveille but the experienced eye could easily distinguish, by various small signs, that soon the order to go to work would be given. Khromoi's assistant (Khromoi, the mess orderly, had an assistant whom he fed) went off to summon Barracks 6 to breakfast. This was the building occupied by the infirm, who did not leave the zone. An old, bearded artist shuffled off to the C.E.D.[1] for the brush and paint he needed to touch up the numbers on the prisoners' uniforms. The Tartar was there again, cutting across the parade ground with long, rapid strides in the direction of the staff quarters. In general there were fewer people about, which meant that everyone had gone off to some corner or other to get warm during those last precious minutes.

Shukhov was smart enough to hide from The Tartar around a corner of the barracks—the guard would stick to him if he caught him again. Anyway, you should never be conspicuous. The main thing was never to be seen by a camp-guard on your own, only in a group. Who knows whether the guy wasn't looking for someone to saddle with a job, or wouldn't jump on a man just for spite? Hadn't they been around the barracks and read them that new regulation? You had to take off your hat to a guard five paces before passing

---

[1] Culture and Education Department.

him, and replace it two paces after. There were guards who slopped past as if blind, not caring a damn, but for others the new rule was a godsend. How many prisoners had been thrown in the guardhouse because of that hat business? Oh no, better to stand around the corner.

The Tartar passed by, and now Shukhov finally decided to go to the dispensary. But suddenly he remembered that the tall Lett in Barracks 7 had told him to come and buy a couple of glasses of home-grown tobacco that morning before they went out to work, something Shukhov had clean forgotten in all the excitement. The Lett had received a parcel the previous evening, and who knew but that by tomorrow none of the tobacco would be left, and then he'd have to wait a month for another parcel. The Lett's tobacco was good stuff, strong and fragrant, grayish-brown.

Shukhov stamped his feet in vexation. Should he turn back and go to the Lett? But it was such a short distance to the dispensary and he jogged on. The snow creaked audibly underfoot as he approached the door.

Inside, the corridor was, as usual, so clean that he felt quite scared to step on the floor. And the walls were painted with white enamel. And all the furniture was white.

The surgery doors were all shut. The doctors must still be in bed. The man on duty was a medical assistant—a young man called Kolya Vdovushkin. He was seated at a clean little table, wearing a small white cap and a snow-white smock. Writing something.

There was no one else in sight.

Shukhov took off his hat as if in the presence of one of the authorities and, letting his eyes shift, in the camp manner, where they had no business to shift, he noticed that Kolya was writing in even, neatly spaced lines and that each line, starting a little way from the edge of the page, began with a capital letter. He realized at once, of course, that Kolya was not doing official work but something on the side. But that was none of his business.

"Well, Nikolai Semyonich, it's like this. . . . I'm feeling sort of . . . rotten . . . ," said Shukhov shamefacedly, as if coveting something that didn't belong to him.

Kolya Vdovushkin raised his big placid eyes from his work. His number was covered up by his smock.

"Why've you come so late? Why didn't you report sick last night? You know very well there's no sick call in the morning. The sick list has already been sent to the planning department."

Shukhov knew all this. He knew too that it was even harder to get on the sick list in the evening.

"But after all, Kolya . . . You see, when I should have come . . . last night . . . it didn't ache."

"And now it does? And what is it?"

"Well, if you stop to think of it, nothing aches, but I feel ill all over."

Shukhov was not one of those who hung around the dispensary. Vdovushkin knew this. But in the morning he had the right to exempt from work two men only, and he'd already exempted them—their names were written down under the glass—it was greenish—on his desk, and he'd drawn a line across the page.

"Well, you ought to have considered that earlier. What are you thinking about? Reporting sick just before roll call. Come on, take this."

He pulled a thermometer out of one of the jars where they stood in holes cut in pieces of gauze, wiped it dry, and handed it to Shukhov, who put it in his armpit.

Shukhov sat on a bench near the wall, right at the very end, so that he nearly tipped it up. He sat in that uncomfortable way, involuntarily emphasizing that he was unfamiliar with the place and that he'd come there on some minor matter.

Vdovushkin went on writing.

The dispensary lay in the most remote and deserted corner of the zone, where no sounds of any sort reached it. No clocks or watches ticked there—prisoners were not allowed to carry watches; the authorities knew the time for them. Even mice didn't scratch there; they'd all been dealt with by the hospital cat, placed there for the purpose.

For Shukhov it was a strange experience to sit in that spick-and-span room, in such quietness, to sit under the bright lamps for five long minutes doing nothing. He cast his eyes around the walls and found them empty. He looked at his jacket—the number on the chest was almost rubbed off. That might be noticed. He ought to have it touched up. He ran his free hand over his chin and felt the stubble. His beard had grown fast since his last bath, over ten days back. But that didn't worry him. Next bath day was about three days off and he'd have a shave then. What was the sense in lining up at the barber's? Who did he have to doll himself up for?

Then as he eyed Vdovushkin's snow-white cap he remembered the hospital on the banks of the River Lovat where he'd been taken with a smashed jaw, and then—what a dope he was!—volunteered for the front again, though he could have lain there in bed for five days.

And now here he was dreaming of being ill for two or three weeks, not dangerously ill, of course, not so bad that they'd have to operate, yet bad enough to go to the hospital and lie in bed for three weeks without stirring; and let them feed him on nothing but that clear soup of theirs, he wouldn't mind.

But, he recalled, now they didn't let you lie in bed even in the camp infirmary. A new doctor had arrived with one of the latest replacements—Stepan Grigorych, a fussy, loud-voiced fellow who gave neither himself nor his patients any peace. He invented jobs in and around the infirmary for all the patients who could stand on their feet—fencing the garden, laying paths, bringing soil to the flowerbeds, and, in wintertime, erecting snow barriers. Work, he said, was a first-rate medicine for any illness.

You can overwork a horse to death. That the doctor ought to understand. If *he'd* been sweating blood laying blocks he'd quiet down, you could be sure of that.

Vdovushkin went on with his writing. He was, indeed, doing some work "on the side," but it was something beyond Shukhov's understanding. He was making a fair copy of a long new poem that he'd finished the previous evening and had promised to show that day to Stepan Grigorych, the doctor who advocated work therapy.

As can happen only in camps, Stepan Grigorych had advised Vdovushkin to describe himself as a medical assistant, and had taken him on at the infirmary and taught him to make intravenous injections on ignorant prisoners, to whose innocent minds it could never occur that Vdovushkin wasn't a medical assistant at all. Vdovushkin had been a university student of literature, arrested while still in his second year. The doctor wanted him to write when in prison what he'd been given no opportunity to write in freedom.

The signal for the roll call was barely audible through the double-paned, frost-blurred windows. Shukhov heaved a sigh and stood up. He still had that feverish chill but evidently he wouldn't be able to skip work.

Vdovushkin reached for the thermometer and read it.

"H'm, neither one thing nor the other. Ninety-nine point two. If it had been a hundred it would have been clear to anyone. I can't exempt you. Stay behind at your own risk, if you like. The doctor will examine you. If he considers you're ill, he'll exempt you. If he finds you fit, he won't. Then you'll be locked up. You'd better go back to work."

Shukhov said nothing. He didn't even nod. Pulling his hat over his eyes, he walked out.

How can you expect a man who's warm to understand a man who's cold?

The cold stung. A murky fog wrapped itself around Shukhov and made him cough painfully. The temperature out there was −17°; Shukhov's temperature was +99°. The fight was on.

He ran at a jog trot to his barracks. The whole parade ground was deserted, the camp looked empty. It was that brief moment of relaxation when, although everything has been decided, everyone is pretending to himself that there will be no march to work. The sentries sit in warm quarters, their sleepy heads propped against their rifles—it's not all milk and honey for them either, lounging on the watch-towers in such cold. The guards at the main gate tossed coal into the stove. The campguards in their room smoked a last cigarette before searching the barracks. And the prisoners, now clad in all their rags, a rope around their waists, their faces bound from chin to eyes with bits of cloth against the cold, lay on their bunks with their boots on and waited, eyes shut, hearts aquake, for their squad leader to yell: "Out you go."

The 104th were with the rest in Barracks 7—all except Pavlo, the deputy squad leader, who moved his lips as he totted something up with a pencil, and Alyosha, Shukhov's clean and tidy neighbor, who was reading from a notebook in which he'd copied out half the New Testament.

Shukhov ran headlong, but without making any noise, straight to Pavlo's bunk.

Pavlo looked up.

"So they didn't put you in the guardhouse, Ivan Deniso-vich? All right?" he asked with a marked Ukrainian accent, rolling out the name and patronymic in the way West Ukrainians did even in prison.

Picking up Shukhov's bread ration he handed it to him. A spoonful of granulated sugar lay in a small mound on top of the hunk. Shukhov had no time to spare but he answered properly (the deputy squad leader was also one of the authorities, and even more depended on him than on the camp commandant). And, though he was in a hurry, he sucked the sugar from the bread with his lips, licked it under his tongue as he put his foot on a support to climb up to make his bed, and took a look at his ration, weighing it in his hand and hastily calculating whether it reached the regulation sixteen ounces. He had drawn many a thousand of these rations in prisons and camps, and though he'd never had an opportunity to weigh them on scales, and although, being a man of timid nature, he knew no way of standing up for his rights, he, like every other prisoner, had discovered long ago that honest weight was never to be found in the bread-cutting. There was short weight in every ration. The only point was how short. So every day you took a look to soothe your soul—today, maybe, they haven't snitched any.

He decided he was half an ounce short as he broke the bread in two. One half he stuck into a little clean pocket he'd specially sewn under his jacket (at the factory they make jackets for prisoners without pockets). The other half, which he'd saved by going without at breakfast, he considered eating on the spot. But food gulped down is no food at all; it's wasted; it gives you no feeling of fullness. He started

to put the bread into his locker but again thought better of it
—he recalled that two barrack orderlies had been beaten up
for stealing. The barracks was a big place, like a public yard.

And so, still clutching the hunk of bread, he drew his feet
out of his valenki, deftly leaving inside them his foot rags
and spoon, crawled barefoot up to his bunk, widened a little
hole in the mattress, and there, amidst the sawdust, concealed his half-ration. He pulled off his hat, drew out of it
a needle and thread (hidden deeply, for they fingered the
hats when they frisked you; once a guard had pricked his
finger and almost broken Shukhov's skull in his rage). Stitch,
stitch, stitch, and the little tear in the mattress was mended,
with the bread concealed under it. Meanwhile the sugar in
his mouth had melted. Every nerve was strained to breaking
point. At any moment the roster guard would begin shouting at the door. Shukhov's fingers worked fast but his mind,
planning the next move, worked faster.

Alyosha the Baptist was reading the Testament under his
breath (perhaps especially for Shukhov—those fellows were
fond of recruiting).

"If you suffer, it must not be for murder, theft, or sorcery,
nor for infringing the rights of others. But if anyone suffers
as a Christian, he should feel it no disgrace, but confess that
name to the honor of God."

Alyosha was smart—he'd made a chink in the wall and
hidden the little book in it, and it had survived every search.

With the same rapid movements as before, Shukhov hung
up his coat on a crossbeam and pulled what he wanted from

under the mattress: a pair of mittens, a second pair of old foot rags, a length of rope, and a piece of cloth with tapes at each end. He smoothed the sawdust in the mattress (it was lumpy and dense), tucked in the blanket, arranged the pillow, and slid down onto his bare feet and started binding them with the rags, first with the good ones, then, on top, with the torn.

Just then Tiurin stood up and barked: "Sleep's over, One hundred and fourth! Out you go."

And at once the entire squad, drowsing or not, got up, yawned, and went to the door. Tiurin had been in for nineteen years and never turned his men out for the roll call a moment too soon. When he said, "Out you go," it meant you'd better.

And while the men with heavy tread and tight lips walked into the corridor one by one and then onto the porch, and the leader of the 20th, following Tiurin's example, called in turn "Out you go," Shukhov drew his valenki over the double thickness of foot rags, slipped his coat over his wadded jacket, and fastened a rope tightly around him (leather belts had been removed from zeks who had them—leather belts weren't allowed in "special" camps).

So Shukhov managed to get everything done and to catch up with the last of his companions, just as their numbered backs were passing through the door onto the porch. Looking rather bulky, for they had wrapped themselves up in every garment they possessed, the men shuffled diagonally toward the parade ground in single file, making no attempt to overtake one another. The only sound was the crunch of their heavy tread on the snow.

It was still dark, though in the east the sky was beginning to glow with a greenish tint. A light but piercing breeze came to meet them from the rising sun.

There is nothing as bitter as this moment when you go out to the morning roll call—in the dark, in the cold, with a hungry belly, to face a whole day of work. You lose your tongue. You lose all desire to speak to anyone.

A junior guard was rushing around the parade ground.

"Well, Tiurin, how long do we have to wait for you? Late again?"

Maybe Shukhov might get scared of him but not Tiurin, oh no. He wouldn't waste breath on him in the cold. Just stomped on in silence.

And the squad followed him through the snow. Shuffle, shuffle, squeak, squeak.

Tiurin must have greased them with that pound of salt pork, for the 104th had gone back to its old place in the column—that could be seen from the neighboring squads. So one of the poorer and stupider squads was being sent to the Socialist Way of Life settlement. Oh, it'd be cruel there today: seventeen degrees below zero, and windy. No shelter. No fire.

A squad leader needs a lot of salt pork—to take to the planning department, and to satisfy his own belly too. Tiurin received no parcels but he didn't go short of pork. No one in the squad who received any lost a moment in taking him some as a gift.

Otherwise you'd never survive.

The senior roster guard glanced at a small piece of board.

"You have one away on sick leave today, Tiurin. Twenty-three present?"

"Twenty-three," said Tiurin with a nod.

Who was missing? Panteleyev wasn't there. But surely he wasn't ill.

And at once a whisper ran through the squad: Panteleyev, that son of a bitch, was staying behind again. Oh no, he wasn't ill, the security boys were keeping him back. He'd be squealing on someone.

They would send for him during the day, on the quiet, and keep him two or three hours. No one would see, no one would hear.

And they'd fix it all up with the medical authorities.

The whole parade ground was black with coats as the squads drifted forward to be searched. Shukhov remembered he wanted to have the numbers on his jacket touched up, and elbowed his way through the crowd to the side. Two or three prisoners stood waiting their turn with the artist. He joined them. They spelled nothing but trouble, those numbers: if they were distinct the guards could identify you from any distance, but if you neglected to have them repainted in time you'd be sure to land in the guardhouse for not taking care of your number.

There were three artists in the camp. They painted pictures for the authorities free of charge, and in addition took turns appearing at roll call to touch up the numbers. Today it was the turn of an old man with a gray beard. When he painted the number on your hat with his brush it was just like a priest anointing your brow.

The old man painted on and on, blowing from time to time into his glove. It was a thin, knitted glove. His hand grew stiff with cold. He only just managed to paint the numbers.

He touched up the S 854 on Shukhov's jacket, and Shukhov, holding his rope belt in his hand and without bothering to pull his coat around him—very soon he'd be frisked—caught up with the squad. At once he noticed that his fellow squad member Tsezar was smoking, and smoking a cigarette, not a pipe. That meant he might be able to cadge a smoke. But he didn't ask straight away; he stood quite close up to Tsezar and, half turning, looked past him.

He looked past him and seemed indifferent, but he noticed that after each puff (Tsezar inhaled at rare intervals, thoughtfully) a thin ring of glowing ash crept down the cigarette, reducing its length as it moved stealthily to the cigarette holder.

Fetiukov, that jackal, had come up closer too and now stood opposite Tsezar, watching his mouth with blazing eyes.

Shukhov had finished his last pinch of tobacco and saw no prospects of acquiring any more before evening. Every nerve in his body was taut, all his longing was concentrated in that cigarette butt—which meant more to him now, it seemed, than freedom itself—but he would never lower himself like that Fetiukov, he would never look at a man's mouth.

Tsezar was a hodgepodge of nationalities: Greek, Jew, Gypsy—you couldn't make out which. He was still young. He'd made films. But he hadn't finished his first when they arrested him. He wore a dark, thick, tangled mustache. They hadn't shaved it off in the camp because that was the way he looked in the photograph in his dossier.

"Tsezar Markovich," slobbered Fetiukov, unable to restrain himself. "Give us a puff."

His face twitched with greedy desire.

Tsezar slightly raised the lids that drooped low over his black eyes and looked at Fetiukov. It was because he didn't want to be interrupted while smoking and asked for a puff that he had taken up a pipe. He didn't begrudge the tobacco; he resented the interruption in his chain of thought. He smoked to stimulate his mind and to set his ideas flowing. But the moment he lighted a cigarette he read in several pairs of eyes an unspoken plea for the butt.

Tsezar turned to Shukhov and said: "Take it, Ivan Denisovich."

And with his thumb he pushed the smoldering cigarette butt out of the short amber holder.

Shukhov started (though it was exactly what he had expected of Tsezar) and gratefully hurried to take the butt with one hand, while slipping the other hand under it to prevent it from dropping. He didn't resent the fact that Tsezar felt squeamish about letting him finish the cigarette in the holder (some had clean mouths, some had foul) and he didn't burn his hardened fingers as they touched the glowing end. The main thing was, he had cut out that jackal Fetiukov, and now could go on drawing in smoke until his lips were scorched. Mmm. The smoke crept and flowed through his whole hungry body, making his head and feet respond to it.

Just at that blissful moment he heard a shout:

"They're stripping our undershirts off us."

Such was a prisoner's life. Shukhov had grown accustomed to it. All you could do was to look out they didn't leap at your throat.

But why the undershirts? The camp commandant himself had issued them. No, something was wrong.

There were still squads ahead of them before it was their turn to be frisked. Everyone in the 104th looked about. They saw Lieutenant Volkovoi, the security chief, stride out of the staff quarters and shout something to the guards. And the guards who, when Volkovoi wasn't around, carried out the frisking perfunctorily, now flung themselves into their work with savage zeal.

"Unbutton your shirts," the sergeant shouted.

Volkovoi was as unpopular with the prisoners as with the guards—even the camp commandant was said to be afraid of him. God had named the bastard appropriately.[1] He was a wolf indeed, and looked it. He was dark, tall, with a scowl, very quick in his movements. He'd turn up from behind a barracks with a "What's going on here?" There was no hiding from him. At first, in '49, he'd been in the habit of carrying a whip of plaited leather, as thick as his forearm. He was said to have used it for flogging in the cells. Or when the prisoners would be standing in a group near a barracks at the evening count, he'd slink up from behind and lash out at someone's neck with a "Why aren't you standing in line, slobs?" The men would dash away in a wave. Stung by the

[1] *Volk* means wolf in Russian.

blow, his victim would put a hand to his neck and wipe away the blood, but he'd hold his tongue, for fear of the cells.

Now, for some reason, Volkovoi had stopped carrying his whip.

When the weather was cold the guards were fairly lenient in the morning, though not in the evening. The prisoners untied their belts, and flung their coats wide open. They advanced five abreast, and five guards stood waiting to frisk them. The guards slapped their hands down the belted jackets, ran over the right pants pocket, the only one permitted by regulation, and, reluctant to pull off their gloves, felt any object that puzzled them, asking lazily: "What's that?"

What was there to look for on a prisoner at the morning roll call? A knife? But knives weren't taken out of the camp, they were brought into it. In the morning they had to make certain a prisoner wasn't taking six pounds of bread with him, meaning to escape with it. There was a time when they were so scared of the quarter-pound hunks the prisoners took to eat with their dinner that each of the squads had to make a wooden case for carrying the whole ration, after collecting it, piece by piece, from the men. What they reckoned to gain by this stupidity was beyond imagining. More likely it was just another way of tormenting people, giving them something extra to worry about. It meant taking a nibble at your hunk, making your mark on it, so to speak, and then putting it in the case; but anyway the pieces were as alike as two peas—they were all off the same loaf. During the march it preyed on your mind: you tortured yourself by imagining that somebody else's bit of the ration might get substituted for yours. Why, good friends quarreled about it, even to the point of fighting! But one day three prisoners escaped in a truck from the work site and took one of those cases of bread with them. That brought the authorities to their senses— they chopped up all the boxes in the guardroom. Everyone carry his own hunk, they said.

At this first search they also had to make sure that no one was wearing civvies under the camp outfit. But, after all, every prisoner had had his civvies removed from him down to the very last garment, and they wouldn't be returned, they were told, until they'd served their terms. No one had served his term in this camp.

Sometimes the guards frisked you for letters that might have been sent through civilians. But if they were going to search every prisoner for letters they'd be fussing around till dinnertime.

Volkovoi, however, had shouted that they were to search for something, and so the guards peeled off their gloves, ordered everyone to pull up his jacket (where every little bit of barrack-room warmth was treasured) and unbutton his shirt. Then they strode up to run their paws over the zeks and find out whether any of them might have slipped on something against the rules. A prisoner was allowed to wear a shirt and an undershirt—he was to be stripped of anything else: such were Volkovoi's instructions, passed down the ranks by the prisoners. The squads that had been frisked earlier were in luck. Some of them had already been passed through the gates. But the rest had to bare their chests. And anyone who had slipped on an extra garment had to take it off on the spot, out there in the cold.

That's how it started, but it resulted in a fine mix-up—a gap formed in the column, and at the gates the escort began shouting, "Get a move on, get a move on." So when it was the turn of the 104th to be frisked they had to ease up a bit: Volkovoi told the guards to take the name of anyone who might be wearing extra garments—the culprits were to surrender them in person to personal property that evening with a written explanation of how and why they had hidden the garments.

Shukhov was in regulation dress. Come on, paw me as hard as you like. There's nothing but my soul in my chest. But they made a note that Tsezar was wearing a flannel vest and that Buinovsky, it seemed, had put on a vest or a cummerbund or something. Buinovsky protested—he'd been in the camp less than three months, a former Navy commander who still couldn't get his destroyer out of his system.

"You've no right to strip men in the cold. You don't know Article Nine of the Criminal Code."

But they did have the right. They knew the code. You, friend, are the one who doesn't know it.

"You're not behaving like Soviet people," Buinovsky went on saying. "You're not behaving like communists."

Volkovoi had put up with the reference to the criminal code but this made him wince and, like black lightning, he flashed: "Ten days in the guardhouse."

And aside to the sergeant: "Starting from this evening."

They didn't like putting a man in the cells in the morning

—it meant the loss of his work for a whole day. Let him sweat blood in the meantime and be put in the cells in the evening.

The prison lay just over there, to the left of the parade ground. A brick building with two wings. The second wing had been added that autumn—there wasn't room enough in the first. The prison had eighteen cells besides those for solitary confinement, which were fenced off. The entire camp was log-built except for that brick prison.

The cold had got under the men's shirts and now it was there to stay. All that wrapping-up had been in vain.

Shukhov's back was giving him hell. How he longed to be in bed in the infirmary, fast asleep! He wanted nothing else. Under the heaviest of blankets.

The zeks stood in front of the gates, buttoning their coats, tying a rope around their bellies. And from outside the escort shouted: "Come on. Come on."

And from behind, the guard urged them on: "Move along. Move along."

The first gate. The border zone. The second gate. Railings along each side near the gatehouse.

"Halt!" shouted a sentry. Like a flock of sheep. "Form fives."

It was growing light. The escort's fire was burning itself out behind the gatehouse. They always lit a fire before the prisoners were sent out to work—to keep themselves warm and be able to see more clearly while counting.

One of the gate guards counted in a loud brisk voice: "First. Second. Third . . ."

And the prisoners, in ranks of five, separated from the rest and marched ahead, so that they could be watched from front and behind: five heads, five backs, ten legs.

A second gate guard—a checker—stood at the next rail in silence, simply verifying the count.

And, in addition, a lieutenant stood watching.

That was from the camp side.

A man is worth more than gold. If there was one head short when they got past the barbed wire you had to replace it with your own.

Once more the squad came together.

And now it was the turn of the sergeant of the escort to count.

"First. Second. Third."

And each rank of five drew away and marched forward separately.

And on the other side of the wire the assistant head guard verified the count.

And another lieutenant stood by and watched.

That was from the side of the escort.

No one dared make a mistake. If you signed for one head too many, you filled the gap with your own.

There were escort guards all over the place. They flung a semicircle around the column on its way to the power station, their machine guns sticking out and pointing right at your face. And there were guards with gray dogs. One dog bared its fangs as if laughing at the prisoners. The escorts all wore short sheepskins, except for half a dozen whose coats trailed the ground. The long sheepskins were interchangeable: they were worn by anyone whose turn had come to man the watchtowers.

And once again as they brought the squads together the escort recounted the entire power-station column by fives.

"You always get the sharpest frost at sunrise," said Buinovsky. "You see, it's the coldest point of the night."

Captain Buinovsky was fond of explaining things. The state of the moon—whether it was old or young—he could calculate it for any day of the year.

He was fading away under your very eyes, the captain, his cheeks were falling in. But he had guts.

Out beyond the camp boundary the intense cold, accompanied by a head wind, stung even Shukhov's face, which was used to every kind of unpleasantness. Realizing that he would have the wind in his face all the way to the power station, he decided to make use of his bit of rag. To meet the contingency of a head wind he, like many other prisoners, had got himself a cloth with a long tape at each end. The prisoners admitted that these helped a bit. Shukhov covered his face up to the eyes, brought the tapes around below his ears, and fastened the ends together at the back of his neck. Then he covered his nape with the flap of his hat and raised his coat collar. The next thing was to pull the front flap of the hat down onto his brow. Thus in front only his eyes remained unprotected. He fixed his coat tightly at the waist with the rope. Now everything was in order except for his hands, which were already stiff with cold (his mittens were worthless). He rubbed them, he clapped them together, for he knew that in a moment he'd have to put them behind his back and keep them there for the entire march.

The chief of the escort guard recited the "morning prayer," which every prisoner was heartily sick of:

"Attention, prisoners. Marching orders must be strictly obeyed. Keep to your ranks. No hurrying, keep a steady pace. No talking. Keep your eyes fixed ahead and your hands behind your backs. A step to right or left is considered an attempt to escape and the escort has orders to shoot without warning. Leading guards, on the double."

The two guards in the lead of the escort must have set out along the road. The column heaved forward, shoulders swaying, and the escorts, some twenty paces to the right and left of the column, each man at a distance of ten paces from the next, machine guns held at the ready, set off too.

It hadn't snowed for a week and the road was worn hard and smooth. They skirted the camp and the wind caught their faces sideways. Hands clasped behind their backs, heads lowered, the column of prisoners moved on, as though at a funeral. All you saw was the feet of two or three men ahead of you and the patch of trodden ground where your own feet were stepping. From time to time one of the escorts would cry: "U 48. Hands behind back," or "B 502. Keep up." But they shouted less and less; the slashing wind made it difficult to see. The guards weren't allowed to tie cloth over their faces. Theirs was not much of a job either.

In warmer weather everybody in the column talked, no matter how much the escort might shout at them. But today every prisoner hunched his shoulders, hid behind the back of the man in front of him, and plunged into his own thoughts.

The thoughts of a prisoner—they're not free either. They keep returning to the same things. A single idea keeps stirring. Would they feel that piece of bread in the mattress? Would he have any luck at the dispensary that evening? Would they put Buinovsky in the cells? And how did Tsezar get his hands on that warm vest? He'd probably greased a palm or two in the warehouse for people's private belongings. How else?

Because he had breakfasted without bread and eaten his food cold, Shukhov's belly felt unsatisfied that morning. And to prevent it complaining and begging for food, he stopped thinking about the camp and let his mind dwell on the letter he'd soon be writing home.

The column passed the wood-processing factory, built by prison labor, the workers' settlement (the huts had been assembled by prisoners too, but the inhabitants were civilians), the new club (convict-built in entirety, from the foundations to the mural decorations—but it wasn't they who saw the films there), and then moved out into the steppe, straight into the wind, heading for the reddening dawn. Bare white snow stretched to the horizon, to the left, to the right, and not a single tree could be seen on the whole expanse of steppe.

A new year, 1951, had begun, and Shukhov had the right to two letters that year. He had sent his last letter in July and got an answer to it in October. At Ust-Izhma the rules had been different: you could write once a month. But what was the sense of writing? He'd written no more often then than now.

Ivan Shukhov had left home on June 23, 1941. On the previous Sunday the people who'd been to Polomnya to attend Mass had said: *War!* At Polomnya they'd learned it at the post office but at Temnenovo no one had a radio in those days. Now, they wrote, the radio roared in every cottage—it was piped in. There was little sense in writing. Writing now was like dropping stones in some deep, bottomless pool. They drop; they sink—but there is no answer. You couldn't write and describe the squad you were working with and what kind of squad leader Andrei Prokofievich was. Just now he had a good deal more to talk about with Kilgas the Lett than with his family at home.

Neither did the two letters a year they sent him throw much light on the way they were living. The kolkhoz had a new chairman—as if that hadn't happened regularly! It'd been amalgamated with neighboring farms—that'd happened before, too, but afterward they'd reduced it to its former condition. And what else? The farmers were failing to fulfill their quota of work days—or the individual plots had been cut down to one-third acre, and some people's right back to the cottage walls.

What he couldn't take in was the fact that, as his wife wrote, the number of people in the kolkhoz hadn't grown by a single soul since the war. All the young men and women, without exception, had managed to get away to work in factories or in the peat-processing works. Half the men hadn't come back from the war at all and, among those who had, were some who cold-shouldered the kolkhoz. They lived in the village and worked on the side. The only men on the farm were Zakhar Vasilych, the manager, and Tikhon, the carpenter, who was turned eighty-four, had married recently, and already had children. The kolkhoz was kept going by the women who'd been there since 1930.

There was something about this that Shukhov couldn't understand—"living in the village and working on the side." He'd seen life in the days of private farming and in the days of the kolkhozes too, but that men weren't working in their own villages—this he couldn't swallow. Sort of seasonal workers, were they? Going out traveling? But then how did the village manage with the haymaking?

They'd given up seasonal work a long time back, his wife had replied. They didn't go out carpentering, for which that part of the country was famous; they didn't make osier baskets, for no one wanted them these days. But they did have a craft, a wonderful new craft—carpet painting. Someone had brought stencils back from the war and from that time it had become so popular that the number of those carpet painters grew and grew. They had no steady jobs, they didn't work anywhere, they helped the kolkhoz for a month or so, just at the haymaking or the harvesting, and for that the kolkhoz gave them a chit saying that so-and-so, a member of the kolkhoz, had been released to carry on his work and that the kolkhoz had no claim on him. And they traveled all over the country, they even flew in airplanes to save time, and they piled up rubles by the thousand and painted carpets all over the place. Fifty rubles a carpet made out of any old sheet you could spare—and it didn't seem to take them more than an hour to make a carpet of it. And Shukhov's wife nursed the strong hope that when Ivan returned he too would become one of those painters. Then they'd raise themselves out of the poverty in which she was living and they'd send the children to a technical school and build a new cottage instead of the old broken-down one. All the carpet painters were building new cottages and now, near the railway station, the cottages had gone up in price from five thousand to all of twenty-five.

Then Shukhov asked his wife to explain to him how he, who'd never been able to draw in his life, was going to become a painter. And what were those beautiful carpets like? What did they have on them? His wife answered that you'd have to be an utter fool not to be able to paint the patterns; all you had to do was to put the stencil on and paint through the little holes with a brush. There were three sorts of carpets, she wrote: the "Troika," an officer of the hussars driving a beautiful troika; the "Reindeer"; and a third with a Persian-style pattern. They had no other designs, but people all over the country were glad to get these and snatch them out of the painters' hands. Because a real carpet cost not fifty but thousands of rubles.

How Shukhov longed to see just one of those carpets!

During his years in prisons and camps he'd lost the habit of planning for the next day, for a year ahead, for supporting his family. The authorities did his thinking for him about everything—it was somehow easier that way. He still had another two winters, another two summers to serve. But those carpets preyed on his mind. . . .

There was easy money to be made, you see, and made fast. And somehow it seemed a pity to lag behind his fellow villagers. . . . But, frankly, he didn't want to turn carpet painter. For that a man needed to be free and easy with people, to be brash, to know how to grease a palm or two. And although Shukhov had trodden the earth for forty years, though he'd lost half his teeth and his head was growing bald, he'd never either given or taken a bribe, nor had he learned to do so in camp.

Easy money weighs light in the hand and doesn't give you the feeling you've earned it. There was truth in the old saying: pay short money and get short value. He still had a good pair of hands, capable hands. Surely, when he was out, he'd find work as a plumber, a carpenter, or a repairman.

Only if they deprived him of his civil rights and he couldn't be taken on anywhere, or if they wouldn't let him go home, would he turn to those carpets for a spell.

Meanwhile the column had come to a halt before the gatehouse of the sprawling site on which the power station stood. While the column was still on the move, two of the escort, clad in ankle-length sheepskins, had left their places and wandered across open country to their distant watchtowers.

Until all the towers were manned the site was forbidden territory. The head guard, a machine gun slung over his shoulder, advanced to the gatehouse. Smoke, a great cloud of it, belched from its chimney—a civilian watchman sat there all night to prevent anyone stealing lumber or cement.

Far in the distance, on the other side of the site, the sun, red and enormous, was rising in haze, its beams cutting obliquely through the gates, the whole building site, and the fence. Alyosha, who was standing next to Shukhov, gazed at the sun and looked happy, a smile on his lips. What had he to be happy about? His cheeks were sunken, he lived strictly on his rations, he earned nothing. He spent all his Sundays muttering with the other Baptists. They shed the hardships of camp life like water off a duck's back.

During the march, Shukhov's face cloth had grown quite wet from his breath. In some spots the frost had caught it and formed an icy crust. He drew it down from his face to his neck and stood with his back to the wind. He'd managed to keep the cold out in most places though his hands were numb in his worn mittens. The toes of his left foot were numb too—that left boot was badly worn. The sole had been repaired twice.

The small of his back ached, and so did the rest of it, all the way up to his shoulders. Ached and throbbed. How could he work?

He looked around, and his eyes fell on the face of the squad leader, who had marched among the last five. Tiurin was a broad-shouldered man, broad in the face too. He looked

morose as he stood there. He had no jokes or smiles for his
squad, but he took pains to see they got better rations. He
was serving his second term; he was a true son of the
GULAG[1] and knew camp ways through and through.

In camp the squad leader is everything: a good one will
give you a second life; a bad one will put you in your coffin.
Shukhov had known Andrei Tiurin since the time they met
at Ust-Izhma, though he hadn't been in his squad then. And
when the prisoners who were in under Article 58[2] were
transferred from general camps to "special" ones, Tiurin had
immediately picked him out for his squad. Shukhov had no
dealings with the camp commandant or the P.P.D., with
foremen or engineers—that was the squad leader's job: he'd
protect him with his own chest of steel. In return, Tiurin had
only to lift an eyebrow or beckon with a finger—and you ran
and did what he wanted. You can cheat anyone you like in
camp, but not your squad leader. Then you'll live.

Shukhov would have liked to ask Tiurin whether they
were to work at the same place as the day before or go somewhere else, but he was afraid to interrupt his lofty thoughts.
He'd only just averted the danger of the squad being sent to
work at the Socialist Way of Life settlement, and now he was
probably deliberating over the "percentage"[3] on which the
squad's rations for the next five days depended.

[1] Central Camp Administration: here used to mean camps in general.
[2] For political crimes.
[3] A paper stating the amount of work done and the percentage of the
plan it amounts to.

Tiurin was heavily pockmarked. He was facing the wind but not a muscle moved—his skin was as tough as the bark of an oak.

In the column the prisoners were clapping their hands and stamping their feet. The wind was nasty. It looked now as if the sentries, known to the prisoners as "parrots," were perched in all six watchtowers, but still they weren't letting the column in. They tormented the life out of you with their vigilance.

Here they are. The head guard came out of the gatehouse with the work checker. They posted themselves on each side of the gate. The gates swung wide open.

"Form fives. First. Second. Third . . ."

The prisoners marched as though on parade, almost in step. To get inside, that was all they wanted—there no one had to teach them what to do.

Just beyond the gatehouse was the office; near it stood the work superintendent, beckoning the squad leaders to turn in there, not that they didn't head that way anyway. Der, too, was there, a convict himself but a foreman, the swine, who treated his fellow prisoners worse than dogs.

Eight o'clock. Five minutes past (the whistle had just sounded the hour). The authorities were afraid that the prisoners might waste time and scatter into warm corners—and the prisoners had a long day ahead of them, there was time enough for everything. Everyone who steps onto the building site bends to pick up a scrap of firewood here and there—fuel for the stove. And they hoard it away in nooks and crannies.

Tiurin ordered Pavlo to go with him to the office. Tsezar turned in there too. Tsezar was well off. Two parcels a month. He greased every palm that had to be greased, and worked in the office in a cushy job, as assistant to the rate inspector.

The rest of the squad at once turned off to the side and vanished.

The sun rose red and hazy over the deserted area. At one place the panels of the prefabs lay under the snow; at another a start had been made on the brickwork, and abandoned when no higher than the foundations. Here lay a broken steam shovel, there a dredge, farther on a pile of scrap metal. A network of ditches and trenches crisscrossed the site with a hole or two here and there. The building of the automobile repair shop was ready for roofing. On a rise stood the power station itself, built up to the second story.

Now there was not a soul in sight. Only the six sentries on their watchtowers were visible—and some people bustling around the office. That moment belonged to the prisoners. The senior work superintendent, it was said, had long been threatening to save time by giving the squads their work assignments the evening before, but for all his efforts they never got around to it—because between the evening and the following morning all their plans turned upside down.

So that moment still belonged to the prisoners. While the authorities were sorting things out you stuck to the warmest place you could find. Sit down, take a rest, you'll have time enough to sweat blood. Good if you can get near a stove. Unwrap your footrags and warm them a little. Then your feet will keep warm all day. And even without a stove it's good to sit down.

The 104th went into a big room in the repair shop where the windows had been glazed during the autumn and the 38th were pouring slabs of concrete. Some of the slabs lay in wooden forms, others, with mesh reinforcement, were stood up on end. The ceiling was high, the floor was of bare earth: a cold place it would've been if they hadn't heated it with lots of coal—not for the sake of the men working there, of course, but to help the slabs set faster. There was even a thermometer, and on Sundays, if for some reason or other no one was sent from the camp to work there, a civilian kept the stove going.

The 38th, naturally, wouldn't let any stranger near their stove. Their own men sat around it, drying their footrags. Never mind, we'll sit here in the corner, it's not so bad.

Shukhov found a place for the seat of his wadded trousers —where hadn't they sat?—on the edge of a wooden form, and leaned against the wall. When he did so his coat and jacket tightened, and he felt something sharp pressing against the left side of his chest, near his heart. It was the edge of the hunk of bread in his little inner pocket—that half of his morning ration which he'd taken with him for dinner. He always brought the same amount with him to work and never touched it till dinnertime. But usually he ate the other half at breakfast. This time he hadn't. But he realized he had gained nothing by economizing—his belly called out to him to eat the bread at once, in the warmth. Dinner was five hours off—and time dragged.

And that nagging pain had now moved down to his legs, which felt quite weak. Oh, if he could only get to the stove!

He laid his mittens on his knees, unbuttoned his coat, untied the tapes of his face cloth, stiff with cold, folded it several times over, and put it away in his pants pocket. Then he reached for the hunk of bread, wrapped in a piece of clean cloth, and, holding the cloth at chest level so that not a crumb should fall to the ground, began to nibble and chew at the bread. The bread, which he had carried under two garments, had been warmed by his body. The frost hadn't caught it at all.

More than once during his life in the camps, Shukhov had recalled the way they used to eat in his village: whole pots full of potatoes, pans of oatmeal, and, in the early days, big chunks of meat. And milk enough to bust their guts. That wasn't the way to eat, he learned in camp. You had to eat with all your mind on the food—like now, nibbling the bread bit by bit, working the crumbs up into a paste with your tongue and sucking it into your cheeks. And how good it tasted—that soggy black bread! What had he eaten for eight, no, more than eight years? Next to nothing. But how much work had he done? Ah!

So he sat there, occupying himself with his hunk of bread, while near him on the same side of the room sat the rest of the 104th.

Two Estonians, close as brothers, sat on a flat concrete slab taking turns smoking half a cigarette from the same holder. These Estonians were equally fair, equally tall, equally lean, and had equally long noses and big eyes. They hung onto each other so closely that you'd think one would suffocate unless he breathed the same air as the other. Tiurin never separated them. They shared their food, they slept in adjacent bunks in the top row. And when they stood in the column, waiting for work to start, or turned in for the night, they went on talking to each other in their quiet, deliberate manner. In fact they weren't brothers at all. They first met here in the 104th. One of them, they explained, had been a fisherman on the coast; the other had been taken as a child to Sweden by his parents when the Soviets were established in Estonia. But he'd grown up with a mind of his own and returned to Estonia to complete his education.

Well, it's said that nationality doesn't mean anything and that every nation has its bad eggs. But among all the Estonians Shukhov had known he'd never met a bad one.

The prisoners sat around, some on the slabs, some on forms, some straight on the ground. A tongue doesn't wag in the morning; everyone sat silent, locked in thought. Fetiukov, the jackal, had been collecting cigarette butts (he even fished them out of the spittoons, he wasn't fussy), and now he was breaking them up and filtering the unsmoked tobacco onto a piece of paper. Fetiukov had three children at home but when he was sentenced they'd disclaimed him and his wife had married again. So he got no help from anywhere.

Buinovsky, who kept stealing glances at him, finally

barked: "Hey, you, what do you think you're doing? Picking up all kinds of diseases? You'll get a syphilitic lip that way. Stop it."

The captain was used to giving orders. He spoke to everyone as if in command.

But Fetiukov didn't give a damn for him—the captain got no parcels either. And with a malicious grin on his drooling lips he replied: "You wait, captain. When you've been in for eight years you'll be picking them up yourself. We've seen bigger men than you in the camp. . . ."

Fetiukov was judging by his own standards. Perhaps the captain would stand up to camp life.

"What? What?" asked Senka Klevshin, missing the point. Senka was deaf and thought they were talking about Buinovsky's bad luck during the frisking. "You shouldn't have shown your pride so much," he said, shaking his head in commiseration. "It could all have blown over."

Senka was a quiet, luckless fellow. One of his eardrums had been smashed in '41. Then he was captured; he escaped, was recaptured, and was sent to Buchenwald. There he evaded death by a miracle and now he was serving his time here quietly. If you show your pride too much, he said, you're lost.

There was truth in that. Better to growl and submit. If you were stubborn they broke you.

Alyosha sat silent, his face buried in his hands. Praying.

Shukhov ate his bread down to his very fingers, keeping only a little bit of bare crust, the half-moon-shaped top of the loaf—because no spoon is as good for scraping a bowl of cereal clean as a bread crust. He wrapped the crust in his cloth again and slipped it into his inside pocket for dinner, buttoned himself up against the cold, and prepared for work. Let them send him out now! Though, of course, it would be better if they'd wait a bit longer.

The 38th stood up and scattered—some to the concrete mixer, some to fetch water, some to the mesh reinforcements.

But neither Pavlo nor Tiurin came back to their squad. And although the 104th had been sitting there barely twenty minutes and the working day—curtailed because it was winter—didn't end till six, everyone felt already they'd had a rare stroke of luck—now evening didn't seem so far off.

"Damn it, it's a long time since we had a snowstorm," said Kilgas, a plump, red-faced Lett, gesturing. "Not one snowstorm all winter. What sort of winter do you call this?"

"Yes . . . a snowstorm . . . a snowstorm," the squad sighed in response.

When there was a snowstorm in those parts no one was taken out to work—they were afraid of letting the prisoners leave the barracks. They could get lost between the barrack room and the mess hall if you didn't put up a guide rope. No one would care if a prisoner froze to death, but what if he tried to escape? There had been instances. During the storms the snow was as fine as dust but the drifts were as firm as ice. Prisoners had escaped over them when they topped the barbed wire. True, they hadn't got far.

Come to think of it, a snowstorm was no use to anyone.

The prisoners sat locked in; the coal was delivered late and all the warmth was blown out of the barracks. Flour didn't reach the camp, so there was no bread; and more often than not there was no hot food either. And as long as the storm lasted—three days, four days, even a week—those days were counted as holidays and had to be made up for by work on Sunday.

All the same, the prisoners loved snowstorms and prayed for them. Whenever the wind rose a little, every face was turned up to the sky. Let the stuff come! The more the merrier.

Snow, they meant. With only a ground wind, it never really got going.

Someone edged up to the stove of the 38th, only to be ousted.

Just then Tiurin walked in. He looked gloomy. His squad understood that there was something to be done, and quickly.

"H'm," said Tiurin, looking around. "All present, hundred and fourth?"

He didn't verify or count them because none of Tiurin's men could have gone anywhere. Without wasting time he gave his men their assignments. The two Estonians, Senka and Gopchik, were sent to pick up a big wooden box for mixing mortar nearby and carry it to the power station. They all immediately knew that they were being transferred to the half-completed building where work had been halted in late autumn. The other men were sent with Pavlo to get tools. Four were ordered to shovel snow near the power station and the entrance to the machine room, and inside and on the ramps. A couple of men were sent to light the stove in the machine room, using coal and such lumber as they could swipe and chop up. Another was to drag cement there on a sled. Two were sent to fetch water, two for sand, and yet another to sweep the snow off the sand and break it up with a crowbar.

The only two left without assignments were Shukhov and Kilgas, the leading workers of the squad. Calling them over, Tiurin said:

"Well, look here, boys—" he was no older than they were but he had the habit of addressing them like that—"after dinner you'll be laying cement blocks on the second-story walls, over there where the sixth stopped work last autumn. Now we have to figure how to make the machine room warmer. It has three big windows and the first thing to do is to board them up somehow. I'll give you people to help, but you must figure out what to board them up with. We're going to use the machine room for mixing the mortar, and for warming ourselves too. Unless we keep warm we'll freeze like dogs, understand?"

He'd have said more, maybe, but up came Gopchik, a Ukrainian lad, pink as a suckling pig, to complain that the other squad wouldn't give them the box. There was a scrap going on over it. So off went Tiurin.

Difficult as it was to start working in such cold, the important thing was to get going.

Shukhov and Kilgas exchanged looks. They'd worked as a

team more than once as carpenter and mason, and had come to respect one another.

It was no easy matter to find something to board up those windows with in the bare expanse of snow. But Kilgas said: "Vanya, I know a little place over there where those prefabs are going up, with a fine roll of roofing felt. I put it aside with my own hands. Let's go and scrounge it."

Kilgas was a Lett but he spoke Russian like a native. There'd been a settlement of Old Believers near his village and he'd learned Russian from childhood. He'd been in the camp only two years but already he understood everything: if you don't use your teeth you get nothing. His name was Johann and Shukhov called him Vanya.

They decided to go for the roll, but first Shukhov ran over to where a new wing of the repair shops was under construction. He had to get his trowel. For a mason a trowel is a serious matter—if it's light and easy to handle. But there was a rule that wherever you worked you had to turn in every evening the tools you'd been issued that morning; and which tool you got the next day was a matter of chance. One evening, though, Shukhov had fooled the man in the tool store and pocketed the best trowel; and now he kept it hidden in a different place every evening, and every morning, if he was put to laying blocks, he recovered it. If the 104th had been sent to the Socialist Way of Life settlement that morning, Shukhov would of course have been without a trowel again. But now he had only to push aside a brick, dig his fingers into the chink—and presto! there it was.

Shukhov and Kilgas left the repair shops and walked over toward the prefabs. Their breath formed thick clouds of vapor. The sun was now some way above the horizon but it cast no rays, as in a fog. On each side of it rose pillars of light.

"Like poles, eh?" Shukhov said with a nod.

"It's not poles we have to worry about," said Kilgas casually, "so long as they don't put any barbed wire between them."

He never spoke without making a joke, that Kilgas, and was popular with the whole squad for it. And what a reputation he had already won for himself among the Letts in the camp! Of course, it was true he ate properly—he received two food parcels a month—and looked as ruddy as if he wasn't in camp at all. *You*'d make jokes if you were in his shoes!

This construction site covered an immense area. It took quite a long time to cross it. On their way they ran into men from the 82nd. Again they'd been given the job of chopping out holes in the ground. The holes were small enough—one-and-a-half feet by one-and-a-half feet and about the same in depth—but the ground, stone-hard even in summer, was now in the grip of frost. Just try and gnaw it! They went for it with picks—the picks slipped, scattering showers of sparks, but not a bit of earth was dislodged. The men stood there, one to a hole, and looked about them—nowhere to warm up, they were forbidden to budge a step—so back to the pick. The only way to keep warm.

Shukhov recognized one of them, a fellow from Viatka.

"Listen," he advised him. "You'd do better to light a fire over each hole. The ground would thaw out then."

"It's forbidden," said the man. "They don't give us any firewood."

"Scrounge some then."

Kilgas merely spat.

"How do you figure it, Vanya! If the authorities had any guts do you think they'd have men pounding away at the ground with pickaxes in a frost like this?"

He muttered a few indistinguishable oaths and fell silent. You don't talk much in such cold. They walked on and on till they reached the spot where the panels of the prefabs lay buried under snow.

Shukhov liked to work with Kilgas. The only bad thing about him was that he didn't smoke and there was never any tobacco in his parcels.

Kilgas was right: together they lifted a couple of planks and there lay the roll of roofing felt.

They lugged it out. Now, how were they going to carry it? They'd be spotted from the watchtowers, but that didn't matter: the "parrot's" only concern was that the prisoners shouldn't escape. Inside, you could chop up all those panels into firewood for all they cared. Nor would it matter if they happened to meet one of the guards. He'd be looking about like the others to see what he could scrounge. As for the prisoners, they didn't give a damn for those prefabs, and neither did the squad leaders. The only people who kept an eye on them were the superintendent, who was a civilian, that bastard Der, and the lanky Shkuropatenko, a mere goose egg, a trusty who'd been given the temporary job of guarding the prefabs from any stealing by the prisoners. Yes, it was

Shkuropatenko who was most likely to spot them on the open ground.

"Look here, Vanya," said Shukhov, "we mustn't carry it lengthwise. Let's take it up on end with our arms around it. It'll be easy to carry and our bodies will hide it. They won't spot it from a distance."

It was a good idea. To carry the roll lengthwise would have been awkward, so they held it upright in between them and set off. From a distance it would look as if there were three of them, rather close to one another.

"But when Der notices the felt on the windows he'll guess where it came from," said Shukhov.

"What's it got to do with us?" asked Kilgas, in surprise. "We'll say it was there before. Were we to pull it down or what?"

That was true.

Shukhov's fingers were numb with cold under his worn mittens. He'd lost all sense of touch. But his left boot was holding—that was the main thing. The numbness would go out of his fingers when he started to work.

They crossed the stretch of virgin snow and reached a sled trail running from the tool store to the power station. Their men must have brought the cement along there.

The power station stood on a rise at the edge of the site. No one had been near the place for weeks and the approaches to it lay under a smooth blanket of snow; the sled tracks, and the fresh trails that had been left by the deep footsteps of the 104th, stood out boldly. The men were already clearing away the snow from around the building with wooden shovels and making a road for the trucks to drive up on.

It would have been good if the mechanical lift in the power station had been in order. But the motor had burned out, and no one had bothered to repair it. This meant that everything would have to be carried by hand to the second story—the mortar and the blocks.

For two months the unfinished structure had stood in the snow like a gray skeleton, just as it had been left. And now the 104th had arrived. What was it that kept their spirits up? Empty bellies, fastened tight with belts of rope! A splitting frost! Not a warm corner, not a spark of fire! But the 104th had arrived—and life had come back to the building.

Right at the entrance to the machine room the trough for mixing mortar fell apart. It was a makeshift affair, and Shukhov hadn't expected it to last the journey in one piece. Tiurin swore at his men just for form's sake, for he saw that no one was to blame. At that moment Kilgas and Shukhov turned up with their roll of roofing felt. Tiurin was delighted, and at once worked out a new arrangement: Shukhov was put to fixing the stovepipe, so that a fire could be quickly kindled; Kilgas was to repair the mixing trough, with the two Estonians to help him; and Senka was given an ax to chop long laths with—felt could then be tacked to them, two widths for each window. Where were the laths to come from? Tiurin looked around. Everybody looked around. There was only one solution: to remove a couple of planks that served as a sort of handrail on the ramp leading up to the second story. You'd have to keep your eyes peeled going up and down; otherwise you'd be over the edge. But where else were the laths to come from?

Why, you might wonder, should prisoners wear themselves out, working hard, ten years on end, in the camps? You'd think they'd say: No thank you, and that's that. We'll drag ourselves through the day till evening, and then the night is ours.

But that didn't work. To outsmart you they thought up work squads—but not squads like the ones outside the camps, where every man is paid his separate wage. Everything was so arranged in the camp that the prisoners egged one another on. It was like this: either you all got a bit extra or you all croaked. You're loafing, you bastard—do you think I'm willing to go hungry just because of you? Put your guts into it, slob.

And if a situation like this one turned up there was all the more reason for resisting any temptation to slack. Regardless, you put your back into the work. For unless you could manage to provide yourself with the means of warming up, you and everyone else would give out on the spot.

Pavlo brought the tools. Now use them. A few lengths of stovepipe, too. True, there were no tinsmith's tools, but there was a little hammer and a light ax. One could manage.

Shukhov clapped his mittens together, joined up the lengths, and hammered the ends into the joints. He clapped his hands together again and repeated his hammering. (He'd hidden his trowel in a nearby crack in the wall. Although he was among his own men, one of them might swap it for his own. That applied to Kilgas too.)

And then every thought was swept out of his head. All his memories and worries faded. He had only one idea—to fix the bend in the stovepipe and hang it up to prevent it smoking. He sent Gopchik for a length of wire—hang up the pipe near the window with it; that would be best.

In the corner there was another stove, a squat one with a brick chimney. It had an iron plate on top that grew red-hot, and sand was to be thawed and dried on it. This stove had already been lit, and the captain and Fetiukov were bringing up barrows of sand. You don't have to be very bright to carry a handbarrow. So the squad leader gave such work to people who'd been in positions of authority. Fetiukov had been a big-shot in some office, with a car at his disposal.

At first Fetiukov had spat on the captain, bawled at him. But one punch on the jaw was enough. They got on all right after that.

The men bringing in the sand were edging over to the stove to warm up, but Tiurin drove them off.

"Look out, one of you is going to catch it in a hurry. Wait till we've got the place fixed up."

You've only to show a whip to a beaten dog. The frost was severe, but not as severe as the squad leader. The men scattered and went back to their jobs.

And Shukhov heard Tiurin say to Pavlo: "Stay here and keep them at it. I'm going to hand in the work report."

More depended on the work report than on the work itself.

A clever squad leader was one who concentrated on the work report. That was what kept the men fed. He had to prove that work which hadn't been done had been done, to turn jobs that were rated low into ones that were rated high. For this a squad leader had to have his head screwed on, and to be on the right side of the inspectors. Their palms had to be greased, too. But who benefited, then, from all those work reports? Let's be clear about it. The camp. The camp got thousands of extra rubles from the building organization and so could give higher bonuses to its guard-lieutenants, such as to Volkovoi for using his whip. And you? You got an extra six ounces of bread for your supper. A couple of ounces ruled your life.

Two buckets of water were carried in, but they had frozen on the way. Pavlo decided that there was no sense in doing it like this. Quicker to melt snow. They stood the buckets on the stove.

Gopchik brought along some new aluminum wire, used for electric leads.

"Ivan Denisovich," he said, as he turned it over to Shukhov, "it's good for making spoons. Teach me how to cast them."

Shukhov was fond of the kid. His own son had died young, and the two daughters he had left at home were grown up. Gopchik had been arrested for taking milk to the forest for Bendera's men,[1] and had been given an adult's term of imprisonment. He was like a puppy and he fawned on every-

[1] General in the Soviet Army who betrayed his country in World War II.

one. But he'd already learned cunning: he ate the contents
of his food packages alone, sometimes during the night.

After all, you couldn't feed everyone.

They broke off a length of wire for the spoons and hid it
in a corner. Shukhov knocked together a couple of planks
into a stepladder and sent Gopchik up to hang the stovepipe.
The boy, as nimble as a squirrel, climbed up into the beams,
pounded in a nail or two, slipped the wire around them, and
passed it under the pipe. Shukhov didn't begrudge him his
energy; he made another bend in the pipe close to the end.
Though there was little wind that day, there might be plenty
tomorrow, and this bend would prevent the pipe from smoking. They mustn't forget that it was for themselves that they
were fixing the stove.

Meanwhile, Senka had finished making the laths, and
Gopchik was again given the job of nailing them up. The
little devil crawled about up there, shouting down to the
men.

The sun had risen higher, dispersing the haze. The two
bright columns had gone. It was reddish inside the room.
And now someone had got the stove going with the stolen
wood. Made you feel a bit more cheerful.

"In January the sun warmed the flanks of the cow," Shukhov chanted.

Kilgas finished nailing the mortar trough together and,
giving it an extra smash with his ax, shouted: "Listen, Pavlo,
I won't take less than a hundred rubles from Tiurin for this
job."

"You get three ounces," said Pavlo with a laugh.

"The prosecutor will make up the difference," shouted Gopchik from above.

"Stop that," Shukhov shouted, "stop." That wasn't the way to cut the roofing felt.

He showed them how to do it.

The men crept up to the stove, only to be chased away by Pavlo. He gave Kilgas some wood to make hods, for carrying the mortar up to the second story. He put on a couple more men to bring up the sand, others to sweep the snow off the scaffolding where the blocks were to be put, and another to take the hot sand off the top of the stove and throw it into the mortar trough.

A truck engine snorted outside. They were beginning to deliver the blocks. The first truck had got through. Pavlo hurried out and waved on the driver to where the blocks were to be dumped.

They put up one thickness of roofing felt, then a second. What protection could you expect from it? It was paper, just paper. All the same, it looked like a kind of solid wall. The room became darker, and this brightened the stove up.

Alyosha brought in some coal. Some of them shouted to tip it onto the stove, others not to. They wanted to warm up with the flames. Alyosha hesitated, not knowing whom to obey.

Fetiukov had found himself a cozy corner near the stove and, the fool, was holding his boots right up to the flames. The captain took him by the scruff of the neck and lugged him off to the barrow.

"You haul sand, you bastard."

The captain might still have been on board ship—if you were told to do something you did it. He had grown haggard during the past month, but he kept his bearing.

In the end, all three windows were covered. Now the only light came through the door. And with it came the cold. So Pavlo had the upper half of the doorway boarded up but the lower left free, so that the men, by stooping, could get through it.

Meanwhile three trucks had driven up and dumped their loads of blocks. Now the problem was how to get the blocks up without a mechanical lift.

"Masons, let's go and look around," Pavlo called.

It was a job to be respected. Shukhov and Kilgas went up with Pavlo. The ramp was narrow enough anyhow, but now that Senka had robbed it of its rails you had to make sure you pressed close to the wall if you weren't going to fall off it. And still worse—the snow had frozen to the treads and rounded them; they offered no grip to your feet. How would they bring up the mortar?

They looked all around to find where the blocks should be laid. The men Pavlo had sent up were shoveling the snow from the top of the walls. Here was the place. You had to take an ax to the ice on the old workings, and then sweep them clean.

They figured out how best to bring up the blocks. They looked down. They decided that, rather than carry them up the ramp, four men would be posted down below to heave the blocks up to that platform over there, that another couple would move them on, and that two more would hand them up to the second story. That would be quicker than carrying them up the ramp.

The wind wasn't strong but you felt it. It would pierce them all right when they started laying. They'd have to keep behind the bit of wall that the old crew had begun on; it would give them some shelter. Not too bad—it'd be warmer that way.

Shukhov looked up at the sky and gasped—the sun had climbed almost to the dinner hour. Wonder of wonders! How time flew when you were working! That was something he'd often noticed. The days rolled by in the camp—they were over before you could say "knife." But the years, they never rolled by; they never moved by a second.

When they went down, they found that everyone had settled around the stove except the captain and Fetiukov, who were still hauling sand. Pavlo flew into a rage and sent eight men out at once to move blocks, two to pour cement into the box and mix it with sand, another for water, another for coal. But Kilgas gave his own orders:

"Well, men, we must finish with the barrows."

"Shall I give 'em a hand?" Shukhov volunteered.

"Yes, help them out," said Pavlo with a nod.

Just then they brought in a tank for melting snow. Someone had told the men that it was already noon.

Shukhov confirmed this.

"The sun's already reached its peak," he announced.

"If it's reached its peak," said the captain reflectively, "it's one o'clock, not noon."

"What do you mean?" Shukhov demurred. "Every old-timer knows that the sun stands highest at dinnertime."

"Old-timers, maybe," snapped the captain. "But since their day a new decree has been passed, and now the sun stands highest at one."

"Who passed that decree?"

"Soviet power."

The captain went out with a barrow. Anyway, Shukhov wouldn't have argued with him. Mean to say that the sun up in the sky must bow down to decrees, too?

The sound of hammering continued as the men knocked together four hods.

"All right, sit down awhile and warm yourselves," said Pavlo to the two masons. "And you too, Senka. You can join them up there after dinner. Sit down."

So now they had a right to sit by the stove. Anyway they couldn't start laying the blocks before dinner and there was no point in carrying the mortar up there—it would freeze.

The coals were gradually glowing red-hot and throwing out a steady heat. But you felt it only when you were near them—everywhere else the shop was as cold as ever.

They took off their mittens. All four men held their hands up to the stove.

But you never put your feet near the flame if you're wearing boots. You have to remember that. If they're leather boots the leather cracks, and if they're valenki the felt becomes sodden and begins to steam and you don't feel any warmer. And if you hold them still nearer the flame then they scorch, and you'll have to drag along till the spring with a hole in your boot—getting another pair can't be counted on.

"What does Shukhov care?" Kilgas said. "Shukhov has one foot almost home."

"The bare one," said someone. They laughed (Shukhov had taken his mended boot off and was warming his foot-rags).

"Shukhov's term's nearly up."

They'd given Kilgas twenty-five years. Earlier there'd been a spell when people were lucky: everyone to a man got ten years. But from '49 onward the standard sentence was twenty-five, irrespective. A man can survive ten years—but twenty-five, who can get through alive?

Shukhov rather enjoyed having everybody poke a finger at him as if to say: Look at him, his term's nearly up. But he had his doubts about it. Those zeks who finished their time during the war had all been "retained pending special instructions" and had been released only in '46. Even those serving three-year sentences were kept for another five. The law can be stood on its head. When your ten years are up they can say, "Here's another ten for you." Or exile you.

Yet there were times when you thought about it and you almost choked with excitement. Yes, your term really *is* coming to an end; the spool is unwinding. . . . Good God! To step out to freedom, just walk out on your own two feet.

But it wasn't right for an old-timer to talk about it aloud, and Shukhov said to Kilgas: "Don't you worry about those twenty-five years of yours. It's not a fact you'll be in all that time. But that I've been in eight full years—now that is a fact."

Yes, you live with your feet in the mud and there's no time to be thinking about how you got in or how you're going to get out.

According to his dossier, Ivan Denisovich Shukhov had been sentenced for high treason. He had testified to it himself. Yes, he'd surrendered to the Germans with the intention of betraying his country and he'd returned from captivity to carry out a mission for German intelligence. What sort of mission neither Shukhov nor the interrogator could say. So it had been left at that—a mission.

Shukhov had figured it all out. If he didn't sign he'd be shot. If he signed he'd still get a chance to live. So he signed.

But what really happened was this. In February 1942 their whole army was surrounded on the northwest front. No food was parachuted to them. There were no planes. Things got so bad that they were scraping the hooves of dead horses— the horn could be soaked in water and eaten. Their ammunition was gone. So the Germans rounded them up in the forest, a few at a time. Shukhov was in one of these groups, and remained in German captivity for a day or two. Then five of them managed to escape. They stole through the forest and marshes again, and, by a miracle, reached their own lines. A machine gunner shot two of them on the spot, a third died of his wounds, but two got through. Had they been wiser they'd have said they'd been wandering in the forest, and then nothing would have happened. But they told the truth: they said they were escaped POW's. POW's, you ——ers! If all five of them had got through, their statements could have been found to tally and they might have been believed. But with two it was hopeless. You've put your damned heads together and cooked up that escape story, they were told.

Deaf though he was, Senka caught on that they were talking about escaping from the Germans, and said in a loud voice: "Three times I escaped, and three times they caught me."

Senka, who had suffered so much, was usually silent: he didn't hear what people said and didn't mix in their conversation. Little was known about him—only that he'd been in Buchenwald, where he'd worked with the underground and smuggled in arms for the mutiny; and how the Germans had punished him by tying his wrists behind his back, hanging him up by them, and whipping him.

"You've been in for eight years, Vanya," Kilgas argued. "But what camps? Not 'specials.' You had broads to sleep with. You didn't wear numbers. But try and spend eight years in a 'special'—doing hard labor. No one's come out of a 'special' alive."

"Broads! Boards you mean, not broads."

Shukhov stared at the coals in the stove and remembered his seven years in the North. And how he worked for three years hauling logs—for packing cases and railroad ties.

The flames in the campfires had danced up there, too—at timber-felling during the night. Their chief made it a rule that any squad that had failed to meet its quota had to stay in the forest after dark.

They'd dragged themselves back to the camp in the early hours but had to be in the forest again next morning.

"N-no, brothers, . . . I think we have a quieter life here," he said with his lisp. "Here, when the shift's over, we go back to the camp whether our job's done or not. That's a law. And bread—three ounces more, at least, than up there. Here a man can live. All right, it's a 'special' camp. So what? Does it bother you to wear a number? They don't weigh anything, those numbers."

"A quieter life, do you call it?" Fetiukov hissed (the dinner break was getting near and everyone was huddling around the stove). "Men having their throats cut, in their bunks! And you call it quieter!"

"Not men—squealers." Pavlo raised a threatening finger at Fetiukov.

True enough, something new had started up. Two men, known to be squealers, had been found in their bunks one morning with their throats cut; and, a few days later, the same thing had happened to an innocent zek—someone must have gone to the wrong bunk. And one squealer had run off on his own to the head of the guardhouse and they'd put him inside for safety. Amazing. . . . Nothing like that had happened in the ordinary camps. Nor here, either, up till then.

Suddenly the whistle blew. It never began at full blast. It started hoarsely, as though clearing its throat.

Midday. Lay down tools. The dinner break.

Damn it, they'd waited too long. They should have gone off to the canteen long ago and taken their places in the line. There were eleven squads at work at the power station and there was room in the canteen for only two at a time.

Tiurin was still missing. Pavlo cast a rapid glance around the shop and said: "Shukhov and Gopchik, you come with me. Kilgas, as soon as I send Gopchik to you, bring the whole squad along."

Others took their places at the stove the moment any were vacated. The men surrounded it as though it was a pretty broad. They all crept up to embrace it.

"Come on, don't spend all night with her!" others shouted. "Let's smoke."

They looked at one another to see who was going to light up. No one did. Either they had no tobacco or they were holding onto it, unwilling to let it be seen.

Shukhov went out with Pavlo. Gopchik loped behind like a hare.

"It's gotten warmer," Shukhov said at once. "Zero, no lower. Fine for laying the blocks."

They stole a glance at those blocks. The men had already thrown a lot of them up to the platform and quite a number had been shifted to the floor above.

Screwing up his eyes at the sun, Shukhov checked its position. He was thinking of the captain's "decree."

Out in the open the wind was still having its way and the cold was still fierce. Don't forget, it was telling them, this is January.

The zeks' canteen was no more than a shanty made of

boards nailed together around a stove, with some rusty metal strips over the cracks. Inside, it was partitioned into a kitchen and an eating room. In neither was there a wood floor; it was pitted with the lumps and hollows that the men's feet had trodden into it. All that the kitchen consisted of was a square stove with a soup kettle stuck on top.

The kitchen was run by two men—a cook and a sanitation inspector. Every morning as he left the camp the cook drew an issue of grits from the main kitchen: about one-and-a-half ounces a head, probably. That made two pounds a squad, a little less than a pood[1] for the whole column. The cook didn't much like carrying the sack of grits the two miles himself, so he got a "helper" to carry it for him—better to give the "helper" an extra portion at the zeks' expense than burden his own back. There was water to be carried, too, and firewood for the stove, and these were jobs the cook didn't much like either; so he found zeks to do them instead, for extra helpings at others' expense. What did it matter to him?

Then there was a rule that food must be eaten in the canteen; but the bowls couldn't be left there overnight, they'd have been swiped by civilians, so about fifty, not more, had to be brought in, and quickly washed after use and turned over to the next diners (an extra helping for the man who carried the bowls). To make sure that no one took bowls from the canteen, a man had to be posted at the door; but however careful he might be people took them just the same, either by distracting his attention or talking him into it. So someone

[1] Thirty-six pounds.

else had to go over the whole site to collect the dirty bowls and bring them back to the kitchen. And *he* got an extra helping. And many others got one too.

All the cook himself did was this: he poured the grits into the pot, adding salt; he divided the fat between the pot and himself (good fat didn't reach the zeks, and the rancid all went into the soup kettle, so when there was an issue of rancid fat from the warehouse, the zeks welcomed it as an extra). Another thing he did: he stirred the kasha[1] when it was boiling.

The sanitation inspector had even less to do—he sat and watched: but when the oatmeal was ready he got his helping, as much as his belly would hold. And the cook too. Then the duty-squad leader arrived—the squad was changed every day —to have a taste and decide whether the stuff was good enough for the workers. He received a double portion.

The whistle sounded again. The squad leaders at once lined up, and the cook handed them bowls through the serving window. In the bottom of the bowls lay some oatmeal, how much you didn't ask, or try to judge by the weight. All you got if you opened your mouth was a bunch of swearwords.

The steppe was barren and windswept, with a dry wind in summer and a freezing one in winter. Nothing could ever grow in that steppe, less than nothing behind four barriers of barbed wire. Bread comes only from the bread cutter; oats

[1] Oatmeal.

are threshed only in the warehouse. And however much blood you sweat at work, however much you grovel on your belly, you'll force no food out of that earth; you'll get no more than the damned authorities give you. And you don't even get that—because of the cook and the "help" and all the other trusties in soft jobs. They rob you here, they rob you in camp, they rob you even earlier—in the warehouse. And those who do the robbing don't swing picks. But you—you swing a pick and take what they give you. And get away from the serving window!

Pavlo and Shukhov, with Gopchik bringing up the rear, walked into the canteen. The men stood there so close to one another that you couldn't see either tables or benches. Some ate sitting down but most stood. The men of the 82nd, who'd been digging those holes half a day without a chance of getting warm, had been the first to get in after the whistle; now even after they'd finished eating they didn't leave. Where else could they warm up? The swearing fell off them like water off a duck's back—it was so much more comfortable here than in the cold. Pavlo and Shukhov elbowed their way in. They'd arrived at a good moment: one squad was being served, another was awaiting its turn, and there was only one deputy squad leader near the window. So, they were well ahead of the rest.

"Bowls, bowls," the cook shouted through the window and people hurriedly handed them over. Shukhov was collecting another lot and turning them in, not to get extra oatmeal but to get what was coming to him quicker.

Behind the partition some "helpers" were already washing bowls—for extra oatmeal.

The cook began to serve the deputy squad leaders who stood ahead of Pavlo in the line.

"Gopchik," Pavlo shouted, over the heads of the men behind him.

"Here I am," came Gopchik's thin goatlike bleat from the door.

"Call the squad."

Off he went.

The main thing today was that the oatmeal was good—real oatmeal, the best sort. It wasn't often they had it. More often they got *magara* twice a day. But real oatmeal is filling, it's good.

How often had Shukhov in his youth fed oats to horses! Never had it occurred to him that there'd come a time when his whole soul would yearn for a handful of them.

"Bowls, bowls," shouted the cook.

Now the 104th was in line. That squad leader's deputy, up ahead, got his double helping and bounced away from the window.

This extra helping, too, was at the zeks' expense—but no one objected. The cook gave double helpings to all the squad leaders, and they either ate the extra helping themselves or gave it to their deputies. Tiurin gave his to Pavlo.

Shukhov's job now was to wedge himself in behind a table, oust two loafers, politely ask another prisoner to move, and clear a little space in front of him—for twelve bowls (to stand close together), with a second row of six, and two more on top. Next he had to take the bowls from Pavlo, repeating the number as he did so and keeping his eyes peeled—in case some outsider should grab a bowl from the table. And he had to see he wasn't bumped by someone's elbow so as to upset a bowl—right beside him people were leaving the table, stepping over the benches or squeezing in to eat. Yes, you had to keep your eyes peeled—was that fellow eating out of his own bowl? Or had he wormed his way up to one of the 104th's?

"Two, four, six," the cook counted at the window. He handed out the bowls two at a time—it was easier for him that way; otherwise he might count wrong.

"Two, four, six," Pavlo repeated quietly to himself, there at the window, in Ukrainian, and at once gave the bowls, in pairs, to Shukhov, who put them on the table. Shukhov didn't repeat the numbers aloud—but he counted more sharply than anyone.

"Eight, ten."

Why wasn't Gopchik bringing in the squad?

"Twelve, fourteen," the counting continued.

The kitchen ran out of bowls. Shukhov had a clear view through the window past Pavlo's head and shoulders. The cook put two bowls down on the counter and, keeping his hands on them, paused as though thinking. Must be bawling out the dishwashers. But just then another bunch of dirty bowls was pushed onto the counter. The cook let go of the two clean ones he'd filled and pushed back the pile of dirty ones.

Shukhov left the fourteen bowls he'd already stacked on the table, straddled a bench, took the two filled ones from the counter, and said quietly to Pavlo rather than to the cook: "Fourteen."

"Stop! Where are you taking those bowls?" shouted the cook.

"He's from our squad," Pavlo confirmed.

"'Our squad,' but he's mixed up the count."

"Fourteen," Pavlo said with a shrug. Himself, he wouldn't have swiped the extra bowls, for as deputy squad leader he had to maintain his dignity; but now he was simply repeating what Shukhov had said—he could always blame him for the mistake.

"I've already counted fourteen," the cook expostulated.

"So you did, but you didn't pass them out. You kept your hands on them," Shukhov shouted. "Come and count for yourself if you don't believe us. Look, they're all here on the table."

As he spoke he'd noticed the two Estonians pushing through to him, and he shoved the two bowls into their hands as they passed. And he'd managed to get back to the table to see that all the bowls were in place—the next table hadn't swiped any, though they'd had plenty of opportunity to do so.

The cook's red face loomed large in the window.

"Where are those bowls?" he asked sternly.

"Here they are, at your service," yelled Shukhov. "Move along, scum, you're spoiling his view," he said to someone, giving him a shove. "Here they are, the pair of them." He picked up two bowls from the second row. "Here we have three rows of four, all nice and neat. Count them."

"Hasn't your squad come?" the cook asked, looking suspiciously around the small segment of the canteen he could see through the window—it had been kept narrow to prevent anyone looking into the kitchen and seeing how much was left in the kettle.

"No, none of 'em are here yet," said Pavlo, shaking his head.

"Then why the hell are you taking bowls when the squad's not here?"

"Here they come," yelled Shukhov.

And everyone heard the peremptory shouts of the captain at the door: "Why are you hanging around here?" he yelled, in his best quarter-deck voice. "If you've eaten, beat it and let others in."

The cook muttered something through the serving window. Then he drew himself up, and his hands could again be seen giving out the bowls: "Sixteen, eighteen."

Then he ladled the last portion, a double helping: "Twenty-three. That's all. Next squad."

The men of the 104th pushed through. Pavlo handed them bowls, passing them over the heads of the prisoners sitting at the second table.

In summer five could have sat on a bench, but now, as everyone was wearing thick clothes, four could barely fit in, and even they found it awkward to move their spoons.

Figuring that of the two bowls of oatmeal that had been swiped one at least would be his, Shukhov lost no time in applying himself to his first bowl. He drew his right knee up to his stomach, pulled his spoon ("Ust-Izhma, 1944") from under his boot top, removed his hat, put it in his left armpit, and ran his spoon around the edge of the kasha.

This is a moment that demands complete concentration, as you remove some of the scanty kasha from the bottom of the bowl, put it carefully into your mouth, and swirl it around there with your tongue. But Shukhov had to hurry, to show Pavlo he'd already finished and was waiting to be offered a second bowl. And there was Fetiukov to be dealt with. He had come into the canteen with the two Estonians and had witnessed the whole affair of the two extra bowls. Now he stood there, straight in front of Pavlo, eying the four undistributed helpings as if to say that he ought to be given at least half a helping too.

Young swarthy Pavlo, however, went calmly on with his double portion, and there was no way of telling whether he noticed anyone standing there, or even remembered those extra bowls at all.

Shukhov finished his kasha. He had promised his belly two helpings, so one wasn't enough now to give him the full feeling he normally got from real oatmeal kasha.

He groped in his inside pocket for the scrap of clean rag, found the unfrozen crescent of crust, and meticulously used it to wipe off the last remnant of mush from the bottom of the bowl and any that still clung to the brim. Then he licked the crust clean; then repeated the whole process. The bowl looked now as if it had been washed, with a dull film, nothing more, on the inside surface. He handed it over his shoulder to one of the dish-collectors and sat on, without replacing his hat.

Though it was Shukhov who had swindled the extra bowls, it was for Pavlo to distribute them.

Pavlo prolonged the agony a little longer while emptying his own bowl. He didn't lick it clean; he merely gave a lick to his spoon, tucked it away, and crossed himself. And then, very lightly, he touched—there wasn't room to move—two of the remaining four bowls. It meant he was giving them to Shukhov.

"Ivan Denisovich, take one for yourself and give the other to Tsezar."

Shukhov knew one of the bowls had to be taken to the office for Tsezar, who would never lower himself by going to the canteen or, for that matter, to the mess hall in camp. He knew it, but, all the same, when Pavlo touched the bowls his heart contracted. Could Pavlo be giving him both? And now, as Pavlo spoke, his heartbeat went back to normal.

Without losing any time he leaned over his lawful spoil and began to eat with deliberation, insensitive to the thumps on his back that the zeks in the next squad were dealing him. The only thing that vexed him was that the second bowl might still go to Fetiukov. Fetiukov was a past master at cadging, but he lacked the courage to swipe anything.

Nearby sat Captain Buinovsky. He had long finished his kasha. He didn't know the squad had two extra portions to dispose of. He didn't look around to see how much Pavlo still had left to hand out. He was simply relaxing, warming up. He was not strong enough to rise to his feet and go out into the cold or into that icy warming-up spot. He, like the very people he had just hounded out of the canteen with his rasping voice, was occupying a place he had no right to and getting in the way of the next squad. He was a newcomer. He was unused to the hard life of the zeks. Though he didn't know it, moments like this were particularly important to him, for they were transforming him from an eager, confident naval officer with a ringing voice into an inert, though wary, zek. And only in that inertness lay the chance of surviving the twenty-five years of imprisonment he'd been sentenced to.

People were already shouting at him and nudging him in the back to make him give up his place.

"Captain!" said Pavlo. "Hey, captain."

Buinovsky shuddered as though he was being jerked out of a dream. He looked around.

Pavlo handed him a bowl of kasha. He didn't ask him whether he wanted it.

The captain's eyebrows shot up. He looked at the bowl as at something miraculous.

"Take it, take it," said Pavlo reassuringly, and picking up the last bowl—for the squad leader—went out.

An apologetic smile flitted over the captain's chapped lips. And this man, who had sailed around Europe and navigated the Great Northern Route, leaned happily over half a ladleful of thin oatmeal kasha, cooked entirely without fat—just oats and water.

Fetiukov cast angry looks at Shukhov and the captain and left the canteen.

But Shukhov thought Pavlo had been right. In time the captain would learn the ropes. Meanwhile, he didn't know how to live.

Shukhov still nursed a faint hope that Tsezar would give him his bowl of kasha. But it seemed unlikely, for more than two weeks had passed since Tsezar had received his last package.

After scraping the bottom and rim of the second bowl in the same way as the first, then licking the crust, Shukhov finally ate the crust itself. Then he picked up Tsezar's bowl of cold kasha and went out.

"It's for the office," he said, as he pushed past the man at the door who tried to stop him taking the bowl out.

The office was in a log cabin near the sentry house. As in the morning, smoke was curling out of the chimney. The stove was kept going by an orderly who worked as an errand boy too, picking up a few kopecks here and there. They didn't begrudge him shavings or even logs for the office stove.

The outer door creaked as Shukhov opened it. Then came another door, calked with oakum. Bringing with him a cloud of frosty vapor, he went in and quickly pulled the door shut (so that they wouldn't yell at him: "Hey, you bastard, shut the door").

The office was as hot as a Turkish bath, it seemed to Shukhov. The sun, coming in through the icy windowpanes, played gaily in the room, not angrily as it did at the power station; and, spreading across the broad sunbeam, the smoke of Tsezar's pipe looked like incense in church. The stove glowed red right through. How they piled it on, the devils! Even the stovepipe was red-hot.

In an oven like that you only have to sit down a minute and you're fast asleep.

The office had two rooms. The door into the second one, occupied by the superintendent, was not quite closed, and through it the superintendent's voice was thundering:

"There's an overdraft on the expenses for labor and building materials. Right under your noses prisoners are chopping up valuable lumber, not to mention prefabricated panels, and using them for firewood at their warming-up spots. The other day the prisoners unloaded cement near the warehouse in a high wind. What's more, they carried it up to ten yards on barrows. As a result the whole area around the warehouse is ankle-deep in cement and the men are smothered in it. Just figure the waste!"

Obviously a conference was going on in there. With the foremen.

In a corner near the door an orderly sat lazing on a stool. Beyond him, like a bent pole, stooped Shkuropatenko—B 219. That fathead—staring out of the window, trying to see, even now, whether anyone was pinching some of his precious prefabs! You didn't spot us *that* time, you snoop!

The bookkeepers, also zeks, were toasting bread at the stove. To prevent it from burning they'd fixed up a grill out of wire.

Tsezar was sprawling over his desk, smoking a pipe. His back was to Shukhov and he didn't notice him come in.

Opposite him sat X 123, a stringy old man who was serving a twenty-year sentence. He was eating kasha.

"No, my friend," Tsezar was saying in a gentle, casual way. "If one is to be objective one must acknowledge that Eisenstein is a genius. *Ivan the Terrible,* isn't that a work of genius? The dance of Ivan's guards, the masked *oprichniki!* The scene in the cathedral!"

"Ham," said X 123 angrily, stopping his spoon in front of his lips. "It's all so arty there's no art left in it. Spice and poppyseed instead of everyday bread and butter! And then, that vicious political idea—the justification of personal tyranny. A mockery of the memory of three generations of Russian intelligentsia."

He ate as if his lips were made of wood. The kasha would do him no good.

"But what other interpretation could he have gotten away with?"

"Gotten away with? Ugh! Then don't call him a genius! Call him ——kisser, obeying a vicious dog's order. Geniuses don't adjust their interpretations to suit the taste of tyrants!"

"Hm, hm!" Shukhov cleared his throat. He hadn't the nerve to interrupt such a learned conversation. But there wasn't any sense in standing there, either.

Tsezar swung around and held out his hand for the bowl, not even looking at Shukhov, as though the kasha had materialized out of thin air.

"But listen," he resumed. "Art isn't a matter of *what* but of *how.*"

X 123 struck the table angrily with the edge of his hand.

"To hell with your 'how' if it doesn't arouse any worth-while feeling in me."

Shukhov stood there just as long as was decent for a man who had brought a bowl of kasha. After all, Tsezar might offer him a smoke. But Tsezar had quite forgotten his presence.

So Shukhov turned on his heel and went quietly out. The cold was bearable, he decided. The block-laying wouldn't go too badly.

As he walked along the path he caught sight in the snow of a short length of steel—a bit of a hacksaw blade.

He could conceive of no immediate use for it, but then you can never tell what you might need in the future. So he picked it up and slipped it into his pants pocket. He'd hide it at the power station. Waste not, want not.

The first thing he did on reaching the power station was to take his trowel out of its hiding place and slip it under the length of rope he wore around his waist. Then he took off for the machine shop.

After the sunlight the shop seemed quite dark and no warmer than outside. Sort of clammy.

All the men had crowded near the round iron stove that Shukhov had fixed, or near the one where the sand was steaming as it dried. Those who could find no room around the stoves sat on the edge of the mortar trough. Tiurin was seated against the stove, finishing the kasha that Pavlo had warmed up for him on it. The men were whispering to one another. They were in high spirits. One of them passed the news on to Shukhov: the squad leader had been successful in fixing the work report. He'd come back in a good mood.

What sort of work he'd found and how it had been rated was Tiurin's own business. What in fact had the squad done that first half of the day? Not a thing. They weren't paid for fixing the stoves, they weren't paid for arranging a place to warm up in—they had done that for themselves, not for the building site. But something had to be written in the report. Perhaps Tsezar was helping the squad leader to fix it up properly. It wasn't for nothing that Tiurin looked up to him. A cleverly fixed work report meant good rations for five days. Well, say four. Out of the five the authorities would wangle one for themselves by putting the whole camp onto the guaranteed minimum—the same for all, the best and the worst. Seems to be fair enough: equal rations for all. But it's an economy at the expense of our bellies. Well, a zek's belly can stand anything. Scrape through today somehow and hope for tomorrow.

This was the hope they all went to sleep with on the days they got only the guaranteed minimum.

But when you thought about it, it was five days' work for four days' food.

The shop was quiet. Zeks who had tobacco were smoking. The light was dim, and the men sat gazing into the fire. Like a big family. It was a family, the squad. They were listening to Tiurin as he talked to two or three of the men by the stove. Tiurin never wasted his words, and if he permitted himself to talk, then he was in a good humor.

He too hadn't learned to eat with his hat on, and when his head was bared he looked old. He was close-cropped like all of them, but in the light of the flames you could see how many white hairs he had.

"I'd be shaking in my boots before a battalion commander and here was the regimental commander himself. 'Red Army man Tiurin at your service,' I reported. The commander looked at me hard from under his beetle brows as he asked me my full name. I told him. Year of birth. I told him. It was in the thirties and I was, let's see, just twenty-two then, just a kid. 'Well, Tiurin, who are you serving?' 'I serve the working people,' I replied, with a salute. He blew up and banged both fists on the desk, bang! 'You're serving the working people, you bastard, but what are you yourself?' I froze inside but I kept a grip on myself. 'Machine-gunner, first-class. Excellent marks in military training and polit. . . .' 'First-class! What are you talking about, you ——? Your father's a kulak. Look, this document has come from Kamen. Your father's a kulak and you've been hiding. They've been looking for you for two years.' I turned pale and kept my mouth shut. I hadn't written a line home for a year, to keep them from tracing me. I had no idea how they were living at home, and they knew nothing about me. 'Where's your conscience?' he shouted at me, all four bars on his collar shaking. 'Aren't you ashamed of yourself for deceiving the Soviet Power?' I thought he was going to hit me. But he didn't. He wrote out an order. To have me thrown out of the army at six o'clock that very day. It was November. They stripped me of my winter uniform and issued me a summer one, a third-hand one it must've been, and a short, tight jacket. I didn't know at the time that I didn't have to give up my winter uniform, just send it to them. . . . So they packed me off with a slip of paper: 'Discharged from the ranks . . . as a kulak's son.' A fine reference for a job! I had a four-day train journey ahead of me to get home. They didn't give me a free pass, they didn't provide me with even one day's rations. Just gave me dinner for the last time and threw me off the post.

"Incidentally, in thirty-eight, at the Kotlas deportation point, I met my former squadron commander. He'd been given ten years too. I learned from him that the regimental commander and the commissar were both shot in thirty-seven, no matter whether they were of proletarian or kulak stock, whether they had a conscience or not. So I crossed myself and said: 'So, after all, Creator, You do exist up there in heaven. Your patience is long-suffering but You strike hard.'"

After two bowls of kasha Shukhov so longed to smoke he felt he'd die if he didn't. And, reckoning he could buy those two glassfuls of home-grown tobacco from the Lett in Barracks 7, he said in a low voice to the Estonian fisherman: "Listen, Eino, lend me some for a cigarette till tomorrow. You know I won't let you down."

Eino gave him a hard look and then slowly turned his eyes to his "brother." They shared everything—one of them wouldn't spend even a pinch of tobacco without consulting the other. They muttered something together and Eino reached for his pink-embroidered pouch. Out of it he extracted a pinch of tobacco, factory-cut, placed it in Shukhov's palm, measured it with his eye, and added a few more strands. Just enough for one cigarette, no more.

Shukhov had a piece of newspaper ready. He tore off a scrap, rolled the cigarette, picked up a glowing coal from where it lay at Tiurin's feet—and drew and drew. A sweet dizziness went all through his body, to his head, to his feet, as if he had downed a glass of vodka.

The moment he began to smoke he felt, blazing at him from across the length of the shop, a pair of green eyes—Fetiukov's. He might have relented and given him a drag, the jackal, but he'd seen him pulling one of his fast ones already that day. No—better leave something for Senka instead. Senka hadn't heard the squad leader's tale and sat in front of the fire, poor guy, his head on one side.

Tiurin's pockmarked face was lit up by the flames. He spoke calmly, as if he were telling someone else's story:

"What rags I had, I sold for a quarter of their value. I bought a couple of loaves from under the counter—they'd already started bread rationing. I'd thought of hopping onto a freight train, but they'd just introduced some stiff penalties for that. And, if you remember, you couldn't buy tickets even if you had the money; you had to produce special little books or show travel documents. There was no getting onto the platform either—militiamen at the barrier, and guards wandering up and down the lines at both ends of the station. It was a cold sunset and the puddles were freezing over. Where was I going to spend the night? I straddled a brick wall, jumped over with my two loaves, and slipped into the public toilet. I waited in there for a while. No one was after me. I came out as though I were a soldier-passenger. The Vladivostok-Moscow was standing in the station. There was a crowd around the hot-water faucet, people banging each other's heads with their teakettles. On the edge of the crowd I noticed a girl in a blue jersey—her kettle was a big one. She was scared of pushing through to the faucet. Didn't want her little feet stepped on or scalded. 'Look,' I said to her, 'hang onto these loaves and I'll get your kettle filled fast.' While I was doing so, off went the train. She was holding the loaves. She burst into tears. What was she going to do with them? She didn't mind losing the kettle. 'Run,' I called to her. 'I'll follow you.' Off she went, with me at her heels. I caught up with her and hoisted her onto the train with one arm. The train was going quite fast. I had a foot on it too. The conductor didn't slash at my fingers or shove me in the chest—there were other soldiers in the carriage and he took me for one of them."

Shukhov nudged Senka in the ribs—come on, finish this, you poor slob. He handed him the cigarette in his wooden holder. Let him take a drag, he's all right. Senka, the chump, accepted it like an actor, pressed one hand to his heart, and bowed his head. But, after all, he was deaf.

Tiurin went on:

"There were six, all girls, in a compartment to themselves —Leningrad students traveling back from technical courses.

A lovely spread on their little table; raincoats swinging from coat hangers; expensive suitcases. They were going through life happily. All clear ahead for them. We talked and joked and drank tea together.

"They asked me what coach I was in. I sighed and told them the truth. 'I'm in a special coach, girls, heading straight for death.'"

There was silence in the shop. All you could hear was the stove roaring.

"Well, they gasped and moaned and put their heads together. And the result was they covered me with their raincoats on the top berth. They hid me all the way to Novosibirsk. By the way, I was able to show my gratitude to one of them later—she was swept up by the Kirov wave in thirty-five. She had just about had it, working in a hard-labor team, and I got her fixed up in the tailoring shop."

"Shall we mix the mortar?" Pavlo asked Tiurin in a whisper.

Tiurin didn't hear him.

"I came up to our house at night, through the back garden. I left the same night. I took my little brother with me, took him to warmer parts, to Frunze. I'd nothing to give him to eat, and nothing for myself either. In Frunze some road workers were boiling asphalt in a pot, with all kinds of bums and stray kids sitting around. I sat down among them and said: 'Hey, you guys, take on my little brother as a learner. Teach him how to live.' They took him. I'm only sorry I didn't join the crooks myself."

"And you never saw your brother again?" asked the captain.

Tiurin yawned. "Never again."

He yawned once more. "Well, don't let it get you down, men," he said. "We'll live through it, even in this power station. Get going, mortar mixers. Don't wait for the whistle."

That's what a squad is. A guard can't get people to budge even in working hours, but a squad leader can tell his men to get on with the job even during the break, and they'll do it. Because he's the one who feeds them. And he'd never make them work for nothing.

If they were going to start mixing the mortar only when the whistle blew, then the masons would have to hang around waiting for it.

Shukhov drew a deep breath and got to his feet.

"I'll go up and chip the ice off."

He took with him a small hatchet and a brush and, for the laying, a mason's hammer, a leveling rod, a plumb, and a length of string.

Kilgas looked at him, a wry expression on his ruddy-cheeked face. Why should *he* jump up before his squad leader told him to? But after all, thought Shukhov, Kilgas didn't have to worry about feeding the squad. It was all the same to him if he got a couple of ounces less—he'd manage on his parcels.

Even so, Kilgas stirred himself—you can't keep the squad waiting, he understood, just because of *you*.

"Wait a minute, Vanya, I'm coming too," he said.

"There you go, fathead. If you'd been working for your-self you'd have been on your feet in a hurry."

(There was another reason why Shukhov hurried—he wanted to lay his hands on that plumb before Kilgas. They'd drawn only one from the tool store.)

"Sure three are enough for the block-laying?" Pavlo asked Tiurin. "Shouldn't we send another man up? Or won't there be enough mortar?"

Tiurin knitted his brows and thought.

"I'll be the fourth man myself, Pavlo. You work here on the mortar. It's a big box, we'll put six on the job. Work like this—take the mortar out from one end when it's ready and use the other for mixing some more. And see there's a steady supply. Not a moment's break."

"Ugh!" Pavlo sprang to his feet. He was young, his blood was fresh, camp life hadn't as yet worn him out. His face had been fattened on Ukrainian dumplings. "If *you're* going to lay blocks, I'll make the mortar for you myself. We'll see who's working hardest. Hey, where's the longest spade?"

That's what a squad leader is too. Pavlo had been a forest sniper, he'd even been on night raids. Try and make *him* break his back in a camp! But to work for the squad leader—that was different.

Shukhov and Kilgas came out onto the second story. They heard Senka creaking up the ramp behind them. So poor deaf Senka had guessed where they would be.

Only a start had been made with laying the blocks on the second-story walls. Three rows all around, a bit higher here and there. That was when the laying went fastest. From the knee to the chest, without the help of a scaffold.

All the platforms and trestles that had been there had been swiped by the zeks—some had been carried off to other buildings, some had been burned. Anything to prevent another squad getting them. But now everything had to be done right. Tomorrow they'd have to nail some trestles together; otherwise the work would be held up.

You could see a long way from up there—the whole snow-clad, deserted expanse of the site (the zeks were hidden away, warming up before the dinner break ended), the dark watchtowers and the sharp-tipped poles for the barbed wire. You couldn't see the barbed wire itself except when you looked into the sun. The sun was very bright; it made you blink.

And also, not far away, you could see the portable generator smoking away, blackening the sky. And wheezing, too. It always made that hoarse, sickly noise before it whistled. There it went. So they hadn't, after all, cut too much off the dinner break.

"Hey, Stakhanovite! Hurry up with that plumb," Kilgas shouted.

"Look how much ice you've got left on your wall! See if you can chip it off before evening." Shukhov said derisively. "*You* didn't have to bring your trowel up with you!"

They'd intended to start with the walls they'd been allocated before dinner, but Tiurin called from below: "Hey, men! We'll work in pairs, so that the mortar doesn't freeze in the hods. You take Senka with you on your wall, and I'll work with Kilgas. But to start with, you stand in for me, Gopchik, and clean up Kilgas's wall."

Shukhov and Kilgas looked at one another. Correct. Quicker that way.

They grabbed their axes.

And now Shukhov was no longer seeing that distant view where sun gleamed on snow. He was no longer seeing the prisoners as they wandered from the warming-up places all over the site, some to hack away at the holes they hadn't finished that morning, some to fix the mesh reinforcement, some to put up beams in the workshops. Shukhov was seeing only his wall—from the junction at the left where the blocks rose in steps, higher than his waist, to the right to the corner where it met Kilgas's. He showed Senka where to remove ice and chopped at it energetically himself with the back and blade of his ax, so that splinters of ice flew all about and into his face. He worked with drive, but his thoughts were elsewhere. His thoughts and his eyes were feeling their way under the ice to the wall itself, the outer facade of the power station, two blocks thick. At the spot he was working on, the wall had previously been laid by some mason who was either incompetent or had stunk up the job. But now Shukhov tackled the wall as if it was his own handiwork. There, he saw, was a cavity that couldn't be leveled up in one row; he'd have to do it in three, adding a little more mortar each time. And here the outer wall bellied a bit—it would take two rows to straighten that. He divided the wall mentally into the place where he would lay blocks, starting at the point where they rose in steps, and the place where Senka was working, on the right, up to Kilgas's section. There in the corner, he figured, Kilgas wouldn't hold back; he would lay a few blocks for Senka, to make things easier for him. And, while they were puttering around in the corner, Shukhov would forge ahead and have half the wall built, so that his pair wouldn't be behindhand. He noted how many blocks he'd require for each of the places. And the moment the carriers brought the blocks up he shouted at Alyosha: "Bring 'em to me. Put 'em here. And here."

Senka had finished chipping off the ice, and Shukhov picked up a wire brush, gripped it in both hands, and went along the wall swishing it—to and fro, to and fro—cleaning up the top row, especially the joints, till only a snowy film was left on it.

Tiurin climbed up and, while Shukhov was still busy with his brush, fixed up a leveling rod in the corner. Shukhov and Kilgas had already placed theirs on the edges of their walls.

"Hey," called Pavlo from below. "Anyone alive up there? Take the mortar."

Shukhov broke into a sweat—he hadn't stretched his string over the blocks yet. He was rushing. He decided to stretch it for three rows at once, and make the necessary allowance. He decided also to take over a little of the outer wall from Senka and give him some of the inside instead; things would be easier for him that way.

Stretching his string along the top edge, he explained to Senka, with mouthings and gestures, where he was to work. Senka understood, for all his deafness. He bit his lips and glanced aside with a nod at Tiurin's wall. "Shall we make it hot for him?" his look said. We won't fall behind. He laughed.

Now the mortar was being brought up the ramp. Tiurin decided not to have any of it dumped beside the masons—it would only freeze while being shifted onto the hods. The men were to put down their barrows; the masons would take the mortar straight from them and get on with the laying. Meanwhile the carriers, not to waste time, would bring on the blocks that other prisoners were heaving up from below. As soon as the mortar had been scooped up from one pair of barrows, another pair would be coming and the first would go down. At the stove in the machine room, the carriers would thaw out any mortar that had frozen to their barrows—and themselves too, while they were at it.

The barrows came up two at a time—one for Kilgas's wall, one for Shukhov's. The mortar steamed in the frost but held no real warmth in it. You slapped it on the wall with your trowel and if you slowed down it would freeze, and then you'd have to hit it with the side of a hammer—you couldn't scrape it off with a trowel. And if you laid a block a bit out of true, it would immediately freeze too and set crooked; then you'd need the back of your ax to knock it off and chip away the mortar.

But Shukhov made no mistakes. The blocks varied. If any had chipped corners or broken edges or lumps on their sides, he noticed it at once and saw which way up to lay them and where they would fit best on the wall.

Here was one. Shukhov took up some of the steaming mortar on his trowel and slapped it into the appropriate place, with his mind on the joint below (this would have to come right in the middle of the block he was going to lay). He slapped on just enough mortar to go under the one block. He snatched it from the pile—carefully, though, so as not to tear his mittens, for with cement blocks you can do that in no time. He smoothed the mortar with his trowel and then— down with the block! And without losing a moment he leveled it, patting it with the side of the trowel—it wasn't lying exactly right—so that the wall would be truly in line and the block lie level both lengthwise and across. The mortar was already freezing.

Now if some mortar had oozed out to the side, you had to chop it off as quickly as possible with the edge of your trowel and fling it over the wall (in summer it would go under the next brick, but now that was impossible). Next you took another look at the joint below, for there were times when the block was not completely intact but had partially crumbled. In that event, you slapped in some extra mortar where the defect was, and you didn't lay the block flat—you slid it from side to side, squeezing out the extra mortar between it and its neighbor. An eye on the plumb. An eye on the surface. Set. Next.

The work went with a rhythm. Once two rows were laid and the old faults leveled up it would go quite smoothly. But now was the time to keep your eyes peeled.

Shukhov forged ahead; he pressed along the outside wall

to meet Senka. Senka had parted with Tiurin in the corner and was now working along the wall to meet him.

Shukhov winked at the mortar carriers. Bring it up, bring it up. Steady. That's the ticket. He was working so fast he had no time to wipe his nose.

He and Senka met and began to scoop out of the same mortar hod. It didn't take them long to scrape it to the bottom.

"Mortar!" Shukhov shouted over the wall.

"Coming up!" shouted Pavlo.

Another load arrived. They emptied that one too—all the liquid mortar in it, anyhow. The rest had already frozen to the sides. Scrape it off yourselves! If you don't, you're the ones who'll be taking it up and down again. Get going! Next!

And now Shukhov and the other masons felt the cold no longer. Thanks to the urgent work, the first wave of heat had come over them—when you feel wet under your coat, under your jacket, under your shirt and your vest. But they didn't stop for a moment; they hurried on with the laying. And after about an hour they had their second flush of heat, the one that dries up the sweat. Their feet didn't feel cold, that was the main thing. Nothing else mattered. Even the breeze, light but piercing, couldn't distract them from the work. Only Senka stamped his feet—he had enormous ones, poor slob, and they'd given him a pair of valenki too tight for him.

From time to time Tiurin would shout "Mo-o-rtar," and Shukhov would shout "Mo-o-rtar"—he was shouting to his own men. When you're working all out, you're a sort of squad leader to your neighbors yourself. It was up to Shukhov to keep up with the other pair. Now, he'd have made his own brother sweat to hurry up with the mortar.

At first, after dinner, Buinovsky had carried mortar with Fetiukov. But the ramp was steep and dangerous, and the captain dragged his feet to begin with. Shukhov urged him on gently: "Quicker, captain. Blocks, captain."

Every time Buinovsky came up he worked faster. Fetiukov, on the other hand, grew lazier and lazier. He'd tilt the barrow as he came up, the lousy bastard, so that the mortar would slop out of it and then it'd be lighter to carry.

Shukhov poked him in the back: "Hey, you damn bastard. When you were an overseer I'll bet you made your men sweat."

Buinovsky appealed to the squad leader: "Give me a man to work with. I won't go on working with this ———."

Tiurin agreed. He sent Fetiukov to heave up blocks from below; and made him work, on top of that, where the number of blocks he handled was counted separately. He told Alyosha to work with the captain. Alyosha was a quiet man; anyone could order him about.

"It's all hands on deck, sailor," the captain urged. "See how fast they're laying blocks?"

Alyosha smiled meekly. "If we have to work faster then let's work faster. Anything you say."

And tramped down for the next load.

Thank God for the man who does his job and keeps his mouth shut!

Tiurin shouted to someone down below. Another truckload of blocks had apparently arrived. Not one had been brought here for six months; now they were pouring in. You could work really fast as long as the trucks brought blocks. But this wouldn't go on. Later there'd be a hold-up in the delivery and then you'd stand idle yourself.

Tiurin was bawling out someone else down below. Something about the lift. Shukhov would have liked to know what was up but he'd no time to find out—he was leveling his wall. The carriers came up and told him: a mechanic had come to repair the motor of the lift, and the superintendent of electrical repairs, a civilian, was with him. The mechanic was tinkering with the motor; the superintendent watched.

That was according to the rules: one man works, one man watches.

Good if they fixed the lift now. It could be used for both blocks and mortar.

Shukhov was laying his third row (Kilgas too was on his third), when up the ramp came yet another snoop, another chief—building-foreman Der. A Muscovite. Used to work in some ministry, so they said.

Shukhov was standing close to Kilgas, and drew his attention to Der.

"Pfah!" said Kilgas contemptuously. "I don't usually have anything to do with the bigshots. But you call me if he falls off the ramp."

And now Der took up his post behind the masons and watched them work. Shukhov hated these snoops like poison. Trying to make himself into an engineer, the fathead! Once he'd shown Shukhov how to lay bricks—and given him a belly laugh. A man should build a house with his own hands before he calls himself an engineer.

At Shukhov's village of Temgenovo there were no brick houses. All the cottages were built of wood. The school too was a wooden building, made from six-foot logs. But the camp needed masons and Shukhov, glad to oblige, became a mason. A man with two trades to his credit can easily learn another ten.

No, Der didn't fall off the ramp, though once he stumbled. He came up almost on the double.

"Tiu-u-urin," he shouted, his eyes popping out of his head. "Tiu-u-urin."

At his heels came Pavlo. He was carrying the spade he'd been working with.

Der was wearing a regulation camp coat but it was new and clean. His hat was stylish, made of leather, though, like everyone else's, it bore a number—B 731.

"Well?" Tiurin went up to him trowel in hand, his hat tilted over one eye.

Something out of the ordinary was brewing. Something not to be missed. Yet the mortar was growing cold in the barrows. Shukhov went on working—working and listening.

"What do you think you're doing?" Der spluttered. "This isn't a matter for the guardhouse. This is a criminal offense, Tiurin. You'll get a third term for this."

Only then did Shukhov catch on to what was up. He glanced at Kilgas. He'd understood, too. The roofing felt. Der had spotted it on the windows.

Shukhov feared nothing for himself. His squad leader would never give him away. He was afraid for Tiurin. To the squad Tiurin was a father; for *them* he was a pawn. Up in the North they readily gave squad leaders a second term for a thing like this.

Ugh, what a face Tiurin made. He threw down his trowel and took a step toward Der. Der looked around. Pavlo lifted his spade.

He hadn't grabbed it for nothing.

And Senka, for all his deafness, had understood. He came up, hands on hips. And Senka was built solid.

Der blinked, gave a sort of twitch, and looked around for a way of escape.

Tiurin leaned up against him and said quite softly, though distinctly enough for everyone to hear: "Your time for giving terms has passed, you bastard. If you say one word, you bloodsucker, it'll be your last day on earth. Remember that."

Tiurin shook, shook uncontrollably.

Hatchet-faced Pavlo looked Der straight in the eyes. A look as sharp as a razor.

"Now, men, take it easy." Der turned pale and edged away from the ramp.

Without another word Tiurin straightened his hat, picked up his trowel, and walked back to his wall.

Pavlo, very slowly, went down the ramp with his spade.

Slo-o-owly.

Der was as scared to stay as to leave. He took shelter behind Kilgas and stood there.

Kilgas went on laying blocks, the way they count out pills

at a drugstore—like a doctor, measuring everything so carefully—his back to Der, as if he didn't even know he was there.

Der stole up to Tiurin. Where was all his arrogance?

"But what shall I tell the superintendent, Tiurin?"

Tiurin went on working. He said, without turning his head: "You will tell him it was like that when we arrived. We came and that's how it was."

Der waited a little longer. They weren't going to bump him off now, he saw. He took a few steps and put his hands in his pockets.

"Hey, S 854," he muttered. "Why are you using such a thin layer of mortar?"

He had to get back at someone. He couldn't find fault with Shukhov for his joints or for the straightness of his line, so he decided he was laying the mortar too thin.

"Permit me to point out," Shukhov lisped derisively, "that if the mortar is laid on thick in weather like this, the place will be like a sieve in the spring."

"You're a mason. Listen to what a foreman has to tell you," Der said with a frown, puffing out his cheeks.

Well, here and there it might be a bit on the thin side. He could have used a little more—but only, after all, if he'd been laying the blocks in decent conditions, not in winter. The man ought to have a heart. You've got to show some results. But what was the good of trying to explain? He didn't want to understand.

Der went quietly down the ramp.

"You get me that lift repaired," Tiurin sang out after him.

"What do you think we are—pack horses? Carrying blocks up to the second story by hand."

"They'll pay you for taking them up," Der called back from the ramp, quite humbly.

"At the wheelbarrow rate? Child's play, pushing up a wheelbarrow. We've got to be paid for carrying them up by hand."

"Don't think I'm against it. But the bookkeepers won't agree to the higher rate."

"The bookkeepers! I've got a whole squad sweating to keep those four masons at work. How much do you think we'll earn?" Tiurin shouted, pressing on without a break.

"Mort-ar," he called down.

"Mort-ar," echoed Shukhov. They'd leveled off the whole of the third row. On the fourth they'd really get going. Time to stretch the string for the next row, but he could manage this way too.

Der went off across the open ground, looking haggard. To warm up in the office. Something must have been eating him. But he should have thought a bit before taking on a wolf like Tiurin. He should keep pleasant with squad leaders like that; then he'd have nothing to worry about. The camp authorities didn't insist on his doing any real hard work, he received top-level rations, he lived in a separate cabin—what else did he want? Giving himself airs, trying to be smart.

The men coming up with the mortar said the mechanic and superintendent had left. The motor was past repair.

Very well, haul 'em up by hand.

For as long as Shukhov had worked with machinery the machines had either broken down or been smashed by the zeks. He'd seen them wreck a log conveyer by shoving a beam under the chain and leaning hard on it, to give themselves a breather; they were stacking log by log with never a moment to stretch their backs.

"Damn the whole ——ing lot of you!" shouted Tiurin, warming up.

"Pavlo's asking how you're fixed for mortar," someone called from below.

"Mix some more."

"We've got half a box mixed."

"Mix another."

What a pace they set! They were driving along the fifth row now. They'd had to bend over double when they were working on the first row, but now the wall had risen shoulder-high. And why shouldn't they race on? There were no windows or doors to allow for—just a couple of adjoining blank walls and plenty of blocks. Shukhov should have stretched a string higher but there was no time for it.

"The eighty-second have gone off to hand in their tools," Gopchik reported.

Tiurin looked at him witheringly. "Mind your own business, squirt. Bring some blocks."

Shukhov looked about. Yes, the sun was beginning to set. It had a grayish appearance as it sank in a red haze. And they'd got into the swing—couldn't be better. They'd started on the fifth row now. Ought to finish it today. Level it off.

The mortar carriers were snorting like winded horses. Buinovsky was quite gray in the face. He might not be forty but he wasn't far off it.

The cold was growing keener. Busy as were Shukhov's hands, the frost nipped his fingers through the shabby mittens. And it was piercing his left boot too. He stamped his foot. Thud, thud.

By now he needn't stoop to the wall, but he still had to bend his aching back for each block and each scoop of mortar.

"Hey, boys!" he pestered the men handling the blocks. "You'd better put them on the wall for me. Heave 'em up here."

The captain would gladly have obliged but lacked the strength. He wasn't used to the work. But Alyosha said: "All right, Ivan Denisovich. Show me where to put them."

You could count on Alyosha. Did whatever was asked of him. If everybody in the world was like that, Shukhov would have done likewise. If a man asks for help why not help him? Those Baptists had something there.

The rail clanged. The signal went dinning all over the site and reached the power station. They'd been caught with some unused mortar. Ugh, just when they'd got into the swing of it!

"Mortar! Mortar!" Tiurin shouted.

A new boxful had only just been mixed. They had to go on laying; there was no other way. If they left anything in the box, next morning they could throw the whole lot of it to hell—the mortar would have petrified; it wouldn't yield to a pickax.

"Don't let me down, brothers," Shukhov shouted.

Kilgas was fuming. He didn't like speed-ups. But he pressed on all the same. What else could he do?

Pavlo ran up with a barrow, a trowel in his belt, and began laying himself. Five trowels on the job now.

Now look out for where the rows meet. Shukhov visualized what shape of block was needed there, and shoving a hammer into Alyosha's hand egged him on: "Knock a bit off this one."

Haste makes waste. Now that all of them were racing one another Shukhov bided his time, keeping an eye on the wall. He pushed Senka to the left and took over the laying himself toward the main corner on the right. It would be a disaster if the walls overlapped or if the corner wasn't level. Cost them half a day's work tomorrow.

"Stop!" He shoved Pavlo away from a block and leveled it himself. And from his place in the corner he noticed that Senka's section was sagging. He hurried over to Senka and leveled it out with two blocks.

The captain brought up a load of mortar, enough for a good horse.

"Another two barrowsful," he said.

The captain was tottering. But he went on sweating away. Shukhov had had a horse like that once. He'd thought a lot of that horse but then they'd driven it to death. They'd worked the hide off it.

The top rim of the sun dipped below the horizon. Now, without Gopchik having to tell them, they saw that the squads had not only turned in their tools but were pouring up to the gates. No one came out into the open immediately after the signal—only a fool would go and freeze out there. They sat in the warmth. But the moment came, by agreement between the squad leaders, when all the squads poured out together. Without this agreement, the zeks, a stubborn lot, would have sat each other out in the warmth till midnight.

Tiurin himself realized that he'd cut things too fine. The man in charge of the tool store must be cursing him out.

"Hey," he shouted, "use enough of that——! Carriers! Go and scrape the big box. Throw what's left into that hole there and scatter some snow on it to keep it hidden. You, Pavlo, take a couple of men, collect the tools, and hand them in. I'll send Gopchik after you with the three trowels. We'll use up the last two loads of mortar before we knock off."

Everyone dashed to his job. They took Shukhov's hammer from him and wound up his string. The mortar carriers and the block lifters hurried down into the machine room. They'd nothing more to do up there. Three masons remained on top —Kilgas, Senka, and Shukhov. Tiurin walked around to see how much wall they'd built. He was pleased. "Not bad, eh? In half a day. Without any ——ing lift."

Shukhov noticed there was a little mortar left in Kilgas's hod. He didn't want to waste it, but was worried that the squad leader might be reprimanded if the trowels were handed in late.

"Listen, men," he said, "give your trowels to Gopchik.

Mine's not on the list. So I won't have to hand it in. I'll keep going."

Tiurin said with a laugh: "How can we ever let you out? We just can't do without you."

Shukhov laughed too, and went on working.

Kilgas took the trowels. Senka went on handing blocks to Shukhov. They poured Kilgas's mortar into Shukhov's hod.

Gopchik ran across to the tool store, to overtake Pavlo. The rest were just as anxious to be in time, and hurried over to the gates, without Tiurin. A squad leader is a power, but the escort is a greater power still. They list latecomers, and that means the guardhouse for you.

There was a terrible crowd near the gates now. Everyone had collected there. It looked as if the escort had come out and started counting.

(They counted the prisoners twice on the way out; once before they unbolted the gates, to make sure they were safe in opening them, and again when the gates had been opened and the prisoners were passing through. And if they thought they'd miscounted, they recounted outside the gates.)

"To hell with the mortar," said Tiurin, with a gesture of impatience. "Sling it over the wall."

"Don't wait, leader. Go ahead, you're needed there." (Shukhov usually addressed Tiurin, more respectfully, as Andrei Prokofievich, but now, after working like that, he felt equal to the squad leader. He didn't put it to himself, "Look, I'm your equal," he just knew it.) And as Tiurin strode down the ramp he called after him, jokingly: "Why do these bastards make the work day so short? We were just getting into our stride when they call it off."

Shukhov was left alone now with Senka. You couldn't say much to him. Besides, you didn't have to tell him things: he was the wisest of them all; he understood without need of words.

Slap on the mortar. Down with the block. Press it home. See it's straight. Mortar. Block. Mortar. Block. . . .

Wasn't it enough that Tiurin had told them himself not to bother about the mortar? Just throw it over the wall and —— off. But Shukhov wasn't made that way—eight years in a camp couldn't change his nature. He worried about anything he could make use of, about every scrap of work he could do—nothing must be wasted without good reason.

Mortar. Block. Mortar. Block. . . .

"Finish, —— you," shouted Senka. "Let's get out of here."

He picked up a barrow and ran down the ramp.

But Shukhov—and if the guards had put the dogs on him it would have made no difference—ran to the back and looked about. Not bad. Then he ran and gave the wall a good look over, to the left, to the right. His eye was as accurate as a carpenter's level. Straight and even. His hands were as young as ever.

He dashed down the ramp.

Senka was already out of the machine shop and running down the slope.

"Come on, come on," he shouted over his shoulder.

"Run ahead. I'll catch up," Shukhov gestured.

But he went into the machine shop. He couldn't simply

throw his trowel down. He might not be there the next day. They might send the squad off to the Socialist Way of Life settlement. It could be six months before he returned to the power station. But did that mean he was to throw down his trowel? If he'd swiped it he had to hang on to it.

Both the stoves had been doused. It was dark, frightening. Frightening not because it was dark but because everyone had left, because he alone might be missing at the count by the gates, and the guards would beat him.

Yet his eyes darted here, darted there, and, spotting a big stone in the corner, he pulled it aside, slipped his trowel under it, and hid it. So that's that.

Now to catch up with Senka. Senka had stopped after running a hundred paces or so. Senka would never leave anyone in a jam. Pay for it? Then together.

They ran neck and neck, the tall and the short. Senka was a head taller than Shukhov, and a big head it was too.

There are loafers who race one another of their own free will around a stadium. Those devils should be running after a full day's work, with aching back and wet mittens and worn-out valenki—and in the cold too.

They panted like mad dogs. All you could hear was their hoarse breathing.

Well, Tiurin was at the gates. He'd explain.

They were running straight into the crowd. It scared you.

Hundreds of throats booing you at once, and cursing you up and down. Wouldn't *you* be scared if you had five hundred men blowing their tops at you?

But what about the guards? That was the chief thing.

No. No trouble with them. Tiurin was there, in the last row. He must have explained. Taken the blame on his own shoulders.

But the men yelled, the men swore. And what swearing! Even Senka couldn't help hearing and, drawing a deep breath, gave back as good as he got. He'd kept quiet all his life—but now, how he bellowed! Raised his fists too, ready to pick a fight right away. The men fell silent. Someone laughed.

"Hey, one hundred and fourth," came a shout. "Your deaf guy's a fake. We just tested him."

Everyone laughed. The guards too.

"Form fives."

They didn't open the gates. They didn't trust themselves. They pushed the crowd back from the gates (everyone stuck to the gates like idiots—as if they'd get out quicker that way!).

"Form fives. First. Second. Third . . ."

Each five, as it was called, took a few paces forward.

While Shukhov was recovering his breath he looked up. The moon had risen and was frowning, crimson-faced. Yesterday at this hour it had stood much higher.

Pleased that everything had gone so smoothly, Shukhov nudged the captain in the ribs and said: "Listen, captain, where does this science of yours say the old moon goes afterward?"

"Where does it go? What do you mean? What stupidity! It's simply not visible."

Shukhov shook his head and laughed. "Well, if it's not visible, how d'you know it's there?"

"So, according to you," said the captain, unable to believe his ears, "it's another moon every month."

"What's strange about that? People are born every day. Why not a moon every four weeks?"

"Phaugh!" said the captain and spat. "I've never met a sailor as stupid as you in my life. So where do *you* think the old moon goes?"

"That's what I'm asking you. Where does it go?" Shukhov showed his teeth in a smile.

"Well, tell me. Where does it go?"

Shukhov sighed and said with a slight lisp: "In our village, folk say God crumbles up the old moon into stars."

"What savages!" The captain laughed. "I've never heard that one. Then you believe in God, Shukhov?"

"Why not?" asked Shukhov, surprised. "Hear Him thunder and try not to believe in Him."

"But why does God do it?"

"Do what?"

"Crumble the moon into stars. Why?"

"Well, can't you understand?" said Shukhov. "The stars fall down now and then. The gaps have to be filled."

"Turn around, you slob," a guard shouted. "Get in line."

The count had almost reached them. The twelfth five of the fifth hundred had moved ahead, leaving only Buinovsky and Shukhov at the back.

The escort was worried. There was a discussion over the counting boards. Somebody missing. Again somebody missing. Why the hell can't they learn to count?

They'd counted 462. Ought to be 463.

Once more they pushed everybody back from the gates (the zeks had crowded forward again).

"Form fives. First. Second. . . ."

What made this recounting so infuriating was that the time wasted on it was the zeks' own, not the authorities'. They would still have to cross the steppe, get to the camp, and line up there to be searched. The columns would come in from all sides on the double, trying to be first at the frisking and into the camp. The column that was back first was top dog in the camp that evening—the mess hall was theirs, they were first in line to get their packages, first at the private kitchen, first at the C.E.D. to pick up letters or hand in their own to be censored, first at the dispensary, the barber's, the baths—first everywhere.

And the escort too is in a hurry to get the zeks in and be off for the night. A soldier's life isn't much fun either—a lot of work, little time.

And now the count had come out wrong.

As the last few fives were called forward Shukhov began to hope that there were going to be three in the last row after all. No, damn it, two again.

The tellers went to the head guard with their tally boards. There was a consultation. The head guard shouted: "Squad leader of the hundred and fourth."

Tiurin took half a pace forward. "Here."

"Did you leave anyone behind in the power station? Think."

"No."

"Think again. I'll knock your head off. . . ."

"No, I'm quite sure."

But he stole a glance at Pavlo. Could anyone have dropped off to sleep in the machine shop?

"Form squads," the head guard shouted.

They had formed the groups of five just as they happened to be standing. Now they began to shift about. Voices boomed out: "Seventy-fifth over here," "This way, thirteenth," "Thirty-second here."

The 104th, being all in the rear, formed there too. They were empty-handed to a man, Shukhov noticed; like idiots, they'd worked on so late they'd collected no firewood. Only two of them were carrying small bundles.

This game was played every evening: before the job was over the workers would gather chips, sticks, and broken laths, and tie them together with bits of string or ragged tapes to carry back with them. The first raid on their bundles would take place near the gates to the work site. If either the superintendent or one of the foremen was standing there, he'd order the prisoners to throw down their firewood (millions of rubles had gone up in smoke, yet there they were thinking they'd make up the losses with kindling). But a zek calculated his own way: if everyone brought even a few sticks back with him the barracks would be warmer. Barrack orderlies were issued ten pounds of coaldust a stove and little heat could be squeezed out of that. So the men would break up the sticks or saw them short and slip them under their coats.

The escort never made the zeks drop their firewood at the gates to the work site. For one thing, it would have been an offense to the uniform; and secondly they had their hands on machine guns, ready to shoot. But just before entering the zone several ranks in the column were ordered to throw their stuff down. The escort, however, robbed mercifully—they had to leave something for the guards, and for the zeks themselves, who otherwise wouldn't bring any with them.

So every zek brought some firewood along with him every evening. You never knew when you might get it through or when they'd grab it.

While Shukhov was scouring the ground in search of a few chips, Tiurin had finished counting the squad.

"One hundred and fourth all present," he reported to the head guard.

Just then Tsezar rejoined his own squad from the group of office workers. His pipe was glowing as he puffed away at it; his dark mustache was tipped with frost.

"Well, captain, how'd it go?" he asked.

A man who's warm can't understand a man who's freezing. "How'd it go?" What a damn fool question!

"If you really want to know," said the captain, his shoulders sagging, "worked so hard I can hardly straighten my back."

You might give me something to smoke was what he meant.

Tsezar gave him something to smoke. The captain was the only man in the squad he stuck to. He could unburden his heart to him—to no one else.

"There's a man missing from the thirty-second. From the thirty-second," everybody began to mutter.

The deputy squad leader of the 32nd scurried off with another young fellow to search the repair shops. And in the crowd people kept asking: Who? How? Where? Soon it reached Shukhov's ears that it was the dark little Moldavian who was missing. The Moldavian? Not the one who, it was said, had been a Rumanian spy, a real spy?

You could find up to five spies in each squad. But they were fakes, prison-made spies. They passed as spies in their dossiers, but really they were simply ex-POW's. Shukhov himself was one of these "spies."

But the Moldavian was genuine.

The head of the escort ran his eye down the list and grew black in the face. After all, if the spy were to escape what would hapen to the head of the escort?

In the crowd everybody, including Shukhov, flew into a rage. Were they going through all this for that ——, that slimy little snake, that stinking worm? The sky was already quite dark; what light there was came from the moon. You could see the stars—this meant the frost was gathering strength for the night—and that runty bastard was missing. What, haven't you had your bellyful of work, you miserable idiot? Isn't the official spell of eleven hours, dawn to dusk, long enough for you? Just you wait, the prosecutor will add something.

Odd that anyone could work so hard as to ignore the signal to knock off.

He completely forgot that he'd been working like that himself only an hour ago—that he'd been annoyed with the others for assembling at the gate too early. Now he was chilled to the bone and his fury mounted with everyone else's; were they to be kept waiting another half hour by that Moldavian? If the guards handed him over to the zeks they'd tear him apart, like wolves with a lamb.

Yes, the cold was coming into its own now. No one stood quiet. They either stamped their feet where they stood or walked two or three paces back and forth.

People were discussing whether the Moldavian could have escaped. Well, if he'd fled during the day that was one thing, but if he'd hidden and was simply waiting for the sentries to go off the watchtowers he hadn't a chance. Unless he'd left a trail through the wire the sentries wouldn't be allowed back in camp for at least three days. They'd have to go on manning the towers for a week, if necessary. That was in the regulations, as the oldtimers knew. In short, if someone escaped, the guards had had it; they were hounded, without sleep or food. Sometimes they were roused to such fury that the runaway wouldn't get back alive.

Tsezar was arguing with the captain: "For instance, when he hung his pince-nez on the ship's rigging. D'you remember?"

"Hm, yes," the captain said as he smoked.

"Or the baby carriage on the steps. Bumping down and down."

"Yes. . . . But the scenes on board are somewhat artificial."

"Well, you see, we've been spoiled by modern camera technique."

"And the maggots in the meat, they crawl about like angleworms. Surely they weren't that size?"

"What do you expect of the movies? You can't show them smaller."

"Well, if they'd bring that meat here to camp instead of the fish they feed us and dumped it straight into the kettle, we'd be only too ..."

The prisoners howled.

Three small figures were bursting out of the repair shop. So they'd found the Moldavian.

"Boooo!" went the crowd at the gates.

And they yelled, as the group drew nearer: "Bastard! Idiot! Cow's twat! Lousy son-of-a-bitch!"

And Shukhov joined in: "Rat!"

It's no joke to rob five hundred men of over half an hour.

Ducking his head, the Moldavian ran like a mouse.

"Halt!" a guard shouted. And, noting down "K 460," said: "Where were you?"

He strode over to the man and turned the butt of his rifle at him.

In the crowd people were still hurling curses: "Ass! Louse! Pig!"

But others, seeing the guard make ready to swing his rifle, held their tongues.

The Moldavian could hardly keep on his feet. He backed away from the guard.

The deputy squad leader of the 32nd advanced.

"The damn fool crawled up to do some plastering. Trying to hide from me! Warmed up there and fell asleep."

And he hit the man hard in the face and on the neck, pushing him farther from the guard.

The Moldavian reeled back, and as he did so a Hungarian, one of his own squad, leaped up at him and kicked him hard from behind.

That wasn't like spying. Any fool can spy. A spy has a clean, exciting life. But try and spend ten years in a hard-labor camp!

The guard lowered his rifle.

The head of the escort shouted: "Back from the gates. Form fives."

Another recount, the dogs. Why should they count us now that everything's clear? The prisoners began to boo. All their anger switched from the Moldavian to the escort. They booed and didn't move.

"W-wha-a-at?" shouted the head of the escort. "Want to sit down on the snow? All right, I'll have you down in a minute. I'll keep you here till dawn."

He was quite capable of doing it, too. He'd had them on the snow many a time. "Down on your faces!" And, to the escort: "Release safety-catches!" The zeks knew all about that. They drew back from the gates.

"Back, back!" yelled the escort.

"What's the sense of shoving up to the gates anyhow, you crappers?" men barked from the rear at the men in front as they were shoved back.

"Form fives. First. Second. Third . . ."

Now the moon was shining full. It cast its light all around and the crimson tint had gone. It had climbed a quarter of the way up the sky. The evening was lost. That damned Moldavian. Those damned guards. This damned life.

As the prisoners in front were counted they turned and stood on tiptoe to see whether there were two men or three in the back row. It was a matter of life or death to them now.

Shukhov had the feeling that there were going to be four. He was numb with fear. One extra. Another recount. But it turned out that Fetiukov, after cadging a butt from the captain, had been wandering around and had failed to get into his five in time. So now he'd turned up in the back row as if he were an extra.

A guard struck Fetiukov angrily on the back of the neck.

Serve him right.

So they counted three in the back row. The count had come out right, thank God.

"Back from the gates," shouted a guard at the top of his voice. But this time the zeks didn't mutter—they'd noticed soldiers coming out of the gatehouse and forming a cordon on the other side of the gates.

So they were going to be let out.

None of the foremen was in sight, nor the superintendent, so the prisoners kept their firewood.

The gates swung open. And now the head of the escort, accompanied by a checker, came and stood on the other side, near some wooden railings.

"First. Second. Third . . ."

If the numbers tallied again the sentries would be removed from the watchtowers.

But what a distance they had to tramp along the edge of

the site to reach the towers at the far end of it! Only when the last prisoner had been led off the site and the numbers had been found to agree would they telephone all the towers and relieve the sentries. If the head of the escort had his wits about him he'd put the column on the move right away, for he knew the zeks had nowhere to run to and the sentries would overtake the column. But some of the guards were so foolish, they feared they didn't have enough troops to handle the zeks; so they waited.

They had one of those idiots this evening.

A whole day in that freezing cold! The zeks were already chilled to the marrow; and now to stand around another shivering hour, when work was over! Yet it wasn't so much the cold and the fact that they'd lost an evening that infuriated them; the point was, there'd be no time now to do anything of their own in the camp.

"How is it you happen to know life in the British Navy so well?" Shukhov heard someone in the next five asking.

"Well, you see, I spent nearly a month on board a British cruiser. Had my own cabin. I was attached to a convoy as liaison officer. And imagine—after the war the British admiral —only the devil could have put the idea into his head—sent me a gift, a souvenir as 'a token of gratitude,' damn him! I was absolutely horrified. And now here we are, all lumped together. It's pretty hard to take, being imprisoned here with Bendera's men. . . ."

Strange! Yes, a strange sight indeed: the naked steppe, the empty building site, the snow gleaming in the moonlight.

And the escort guards: they'd gone to their posts, ten paces apart, guns at the ready. And the black herd of prisoners; and among them, in a black coat like all the rest, a man, S 311, who'd never imagined life without gold shoulder straps, who had hobnobbed with a British admiral and now sweated at a barrow with Fetiukov.

You can push a man this way, and you can push a man that way.

Now the escort was ready. This time without any "prayer" the head guard barked at them: "Double time! Get a move on!"

To hell with your "Get a move on!" All the other columns were ahead of them. What sense was there in hurrying? The prisoners didn't have to be in league with one another to figure the score: You kept us back; now it's our turn. The escort too, after all, was dying for a warm corner.

"Step lively!" shouted the guard. "Step lively, you in front."

To hell with your "Step lively." The zeks marched with measured tread, hanging their heads as at a funeral. Now we've nothing to lose—we'd be the last back anyhow. He wouldn't treat us like human beings; now let him burst himself shouting.

On he went, "Step lively! Step lively!" But he realized it was futile. He couldn't order his men to shoot either. The prisoners were marching in fives, keeping in line, all correct. He had no power to hound them faster. (When they marched out to work in the morning the zeks walked slowly, to spare themselves. A man who's in a hurry won't live to see the end of his stretch—he'll tire and be done for.)

So on with regular, deliberate steps. The snow crunched under their boots. Some of them talked in low voices; others walked in silence. Shukhov asked himself whether there was anything he'd left undone in the camp that morning. Ah, the dispensary. Funny, he'd forgotten all about the dispensary while he'd been working.

This must be around the consulting hour. He'd manage it if he skipped his supper. But now somehow his back wasn't aching. And his temperature wouldn't be high enough. A waste of time. He'd pull through without benefit of the doctor. The only cure those docs know is to put you in your grave.

It wasn't the dispensary that appealed to him now; it was the prospect of adding something to his supper. His hopes were all pinned on that long-overdue parcel of Tsezar's.

A sudden change came over the column. It began to sway, to break out of its regular stride. The prisoners heaved forward with a buzz of excitement. And now the last five, which included Shukhov, were no longer treading on the heels of the five in front; they had to run to keep up. A few more paces, and again they were running.

When the rear of the column spilled over a rise Shukhov saw to the right, far away across the steppe, another dark column on the move, marching diagonally across their course. They, too, seemed to be forcing their pace.

It must be from the machine works, that column; there were about three hundred men in it. Another bunch with bad luck! Must have been held up—Shukhov wondered why. To finish assembling some piece of machinery? They could be kept after work hours for that. But what did it matter to them? They worked all day in the warmth.

Who'd get in first? The men ran, just ran. Even the escort broke into a jog trot: only the head guard remembered to shout, "Don't fall back. Keep up there, you in the rear. Keep up."

Oh, shut your trap. . . . What are you yapping about? As if we wouldn't keep up!

They forgot to talk; they forgot to think; everyone in the column was obsessed by one idea: to get back first.

Things were so lumped together, the sweet and the sour, that the prisoners saw the escort itself, now, as friend rather than foe. Now the enemy was the other column.

Their spirits rose, their anger passed.

"Get a move on, get a move on!" the rear shouted to the front.

Now our column had reached the street, while the other had passed out of sight behind the blocks of houses. They'd been racing blindly.

It was easier for us now, we were running down the middle of the street. And our escort had less to stumble over at the sides. This was where we ought to gain ground.

There was another reason why we simply had to reach the camp gates first: the guards there were unusually slow in searching the column from the machine works. Ever since zeks had begun cutting one another's throats in the camp the authorities had arrived at one conclusion: that knives were being made at the machine works and smuggled in. So the zeks who worked there were gone over with special thoroughness on return to the camp. In late autumn, when the earth was already cold, the guards would shout at them: "Off with your boots, machineworks squad! Hold your boots in your hands."

And would frisk them barefoot.

Or, despite the frost, they'd pick men out at random, shouting: "You there, take off your right boot. And you, take off your left!"

A zek would pull off his boot and, hoping on one foot, turn it upside down and shake out the footrag. No knife, damn you!

Shukhov had heard—he didn't know whether it was true or not—that back in the summer the zeks from the machine works had brought back two poles for a volleyball net and that there the knives were, there inside them. Ten long knives in each pole. And now knives would turn up occasionally, here and there.

So it was at a jog trot that they passed the new club and the residential block and the wood-processing plant, and reached the turning that led straight on to the gates.

"Hoooooo-ooo," shouted the whole column, in unison.

That was the turning we'd aimed at reaching before the others. The rival column was a hundred and fifty paces behind, on our right.

Now we could take things easy. Everyone was elated. As elated as a rabbit when it finds it can still terrify a frog.

There lay the camp, just as we'd left it in the morning: lights were on in the zone over the thick fence, specially powerful ones in front of the gatehouse. The entire area was flooded with light; it was as bright as day. They had to have it like that when they frisked us.

But we hadn't reached the gates yet.

"Halt!" shouted a guard and, handing his machine gun to a soldier, ran up close to the column (they weren't allowed to do that with their guns). "All those on the right carrying firewood dump it to their right."

He didn't have to guess about the firewood—the zeks were carrying it quite openly. A bundle fell, a second, a third. Some would have liked to conceal a stick or two inside the column, but their neighbors objected: "Throw it down as you're told! Do you want others to lose theirs because of you?"

Who's the zek's main enemy? Another zek. If only they weren't at odds with one another—ah, what a difference that'd make!

"Double time," shouted the head guard.

They advanced toward the gates.

Here five roads converged. An hour earlier all the other columns had met here. If they were paved, these roads, this would be just the place for the main square of a future city; and then processions would meet here, just as columns of zeks did now as they poured in from every direction, with sentries and guards all about.

The guards were already warming themselves indoors. They came out and formed a cordon across the road.

"Unbutton your coats. Unbutton your jackets."

They pulled the zeks' arms apart, the better to hug them and slap their sides. Same as in the morning, more or less.

It isn't so terrible to unbutton your coat now. We're going home.

That's what everyone used to say: "Going home."

We never had time to think of any other home.

While the head of the column was being frisked, Shukhov went over to Tsezar. "Tsezar Markovich, I'll run straight to the parcels office and keep a place in line for you."

Tsezar turned. The fringe of his dark mustache was tipped with frost.

"Why should you do that, Ivan Denisovich? Perhaps there won't be a parcel."

"Oh, well, it doesn't matter if there isn't. I'll wait ten minutes, anyway. If you don't turn up I'll go to the barracks."

(Shukhov reckoned like this: if Tsezar didn't come, maybe someone else would; then he could sell him his place in line.)

Obviously Tsezar was longing for his parcel.

"All right, Ivan Denisovich, run ahead and keep a place for me. Wait ten minutes, no longer."

And now Shukhov was on the point of being frisked. Today he had nothing to conceal. He would step forward fearlessly. He slowly unbuttoned his coat and undid the rope belt around his wadded jacket, and although he couldn't remember having anything forbidden, eight years in camp had given him the habit of caution: he thrust a hand into his pants pocket to make sure it was empty.

And there lay a small piece of broken hacksaw blade, the

tiny length of steel that he'd picked up in his thriftiness at the building site without any intention of bringing it to camp.

He hadn't meant to bring it, but now, what a pity to throw it away! Why, he could make a little knife out of it, very handy for shoe repairing or tailoring!

If he'd intended to bring it with him he'd have thought hard of where to conceal it. But now the guards were only two rows ahead and the first of these rows was already stepping forward to be searched.

His choice had to be swift as the wind. Should he take cover behind the row in front of him and toss the bit of metal in the snow (it'd be noticed but they wouldn't know who the culprit was) or keep it on him?

For that strip of hacksaw he could get ten days in the cells, if they classed it as a knife.

But a cobbler's knife was money, it was bread.

A pity to throw it away.

He slipped it into his left mitten.

At that moment the next row was ordered to step forward and be searched.

Now the last three men stood in full view—Senka, Shukhov, and the man from the 32nd squad who had gone to look for the Moldavian.

Because they were three and the guards facing them were five, Shukhov could try a ruse. He could choose which of the two guards on the right to present himself to. He decided against a young pink-faced one and plumped for an older man with a gray mustache. The older one, of course, was experienced and could find the blade easily if he wanted to, but because of his age he would be fed up with the job. It must stink in his nose now like burning sulfur.

Meanwhile Shukhov had removed both mittens, the empty one and the one with the hacksaw, and held them in one hand (the empty one in front) together with the untied rope belt. He fully unbuttoned his jacket, lifted high the edges of his coat and jacket (never had he been so servile at the search but now he wanted to show he was innocent— Come on, frisk me!), and at the word of command stepped forward.

The guard slapped Shukhov's sides and back, and the outside of his pants pocket. Nothing there. He kneaded the edges of coat and jacket. Nothing there either. He was about to pass him through when, for safety's sake, he crushed the mitten that Shukhov held out to him—the empty one.

The guard crushed it in his hand, and Shukhov felt as though pincers of iron were crushing everything inside him. One such squeeze on the other mitten and he'd be sunk— the cells on nine ounces of bread a day and hot stew one day in three. He imagined how weak he'd grow, how difficult he'd find it to get back to his present condition, neither fed nor starving.

And an urgent prayer rose in his heart: "Oh Lord, save me! Don't let them send me to the cells."

And while all this raced through his mind, the guard, after finishing with the right-hand mitten, stretched a hand out to deal with the other (he would have squeezed them at the same moment if Shukhov had held them in separate hands). Just then the guard heard his chief, who was in a hurry to get on, shout to the escort: "Come on, bring up the machine-works column."

And instead of examining the other mitten the old guard waved Shukhov on. He was through.

He ran off to catch up with the others. They had already formed fives in a sort of corridor between long beams, like horse stalls in a market, a sort of paddock for prisoners. He ran lightly, hardly feeling the ground. He didn't say a prayer of thanksgiving because he hadn't time, and anyway it would have been out of place.

The escort now drew aside. They were only waiting for their chief. They had gathered for their own use all the firewood the 104th had dumped before being frisked; what the guards had removed during the frisking itself was heaped near the gatehouse.

The moon had risen still higher; the cold grew keener in the pale bright night.

The head guard walked to the sentry house—he had to get a receipt for the four hundred and sixty-three prisoners. He spoke briefly to Priakhov, Volkovoi's deputy.

"K 460," shouted Priakhov.

The Moldavian, who had buried himself deep in the column, drew in his breath and went over to the right of the corridor. He was still hanging his head and his shoulders were hunched.

"Come here," Priakhov ordered, gesturing for him to walk around the column.

The Moldavian did so. He was ordered to stand there, his arms behind his back.

That meant they were going to charge him with attempting to escape. They'd put him in the cells.

Just in front of the gates, right and left of the "paddock," stood two guards. The gates, three times the height of a man, opened slowly. The command rang out:

"Form fives!" (No need here to order the zeks back from the gates; all the gates opened inwards, into the zone. Let the zeks mass as they wished and push against the gates from within, they wouldn't be able to break out.) "First. Second. Third . . ."

It was at the evening recount on their return through the gates that the prisoners, freezing and famished, found the icy wind hardest to bear. A bowl of thin cabbage soup, half burned, was as welcome to them as rain to parched earth. They'd swallow it in one gulp. That bowl of soup—it was dearer than freedom, dearer than life itself, past, present, and future.

They passed through the gates, those zeks, like soldiers back from a campaign, brisk, taut, eager—clear the road for 'em.

For a trusty with a soft job at staff quarters, those prisoners on the march must have been something to think about.

After the recount a prisoner became a free man again—for the first time in the day since the guards had given them the morning signal for roll call. They passed through the big gates (of the zone), through the small gates (of the intermediate zone), through two more gates (on the parade ground)—and then they could scatter where they liked.

But not the squad leaders. They were caught by the officer who assigned them their work: "All squad leaders to the planning office."

Shukhov rushed past the prison, between the barracks, to the parcels office. Tsezar, meanwhile, went at a dignified, even pace in the opposite direction, to where people were swarming around a pole with a board nailed to it. On it was the name of anyone for whom a parcel was waiting, written in indelible pencil.

Most writing in the camp was done on plywood, not on paper. It was surer, somehow, more reliable. The guards and turnkeys used wood, too, for keeping tally of the zeks. You can scrape it clean for next day, and use it again. Economical.

Zeks who stay in camp all day can, among other odd jobs, read the names on the board, meet people who've got a parcel as they come in from work, and give them the number. Not much of a job, but it can earn you a cigarette.

Shukhov ran to the parcels office—a little annex to a barracks, to which in turn a small porch had been added. The porch had no door and was open to the weather. All the same, it was cozier that way; it had a roof, after all.

A line had formed along the walls of the porch, Shukhov joined it. There were some fifteen ahead of him. That meant over an hour's wait, to just before locking-up time. And there were others who'd be behind him in the line—the zeks of the powerhouse column who'd gone to look for their names on the board, and the machine-works column too. Looked as though *they* would have to come again. Tomorrow morning.

People stood in the line with little bags and sacks. On the other side of the door (Shukhov himself hadn't ever received a parcel at this camp but he knew from gossip) guards opened the parcels, which came packed in wooden boxes, with hatchets. They took everything out and examined the contents. They cut, they broke, they fingered. They tipped things out from one container into another. If there was anything liquid, in glass jars or tins, they opened them and poured it out, though you had nothing but your hands or a cloth bag to hold it in. They didn't give you the jars; they were scared of something. If there was anything home-baked, or some tasty sweetmeats or sausage or smoked fish, the guard would take a bite at it himself. (And just you try to get high and mighty and complain, and they'll immediately say that this and that are forbidden and won't issue them to you at all.) Every zek who got a parcel had to give and give, starting with the guard who opened it. And when they'd finished their search they didn't give you the stuff in the box it had come in; they just swept everything into your bag, even into the skirt of your coat and . . . off you go. Sometimes they'd whisk you out so fast you'd be sure to leave something behind. No good going back for it. It wouldn't be there.

When he was in Ust-Izhma Shukhov had got parcels a couple of times. But he wrote to his wife that it was a waste—don't send them. Don't take the food out of the kids' mouths.

Although when he had been at liberty Shukhov had found it easier to feed his whole family than it ever was to feed himself now, he knew what those parcels cost. He knew too that his family wouldn't be able to keep it up for ten years. Better do without them.

But though he'd decided that way, every time someone in the squad, or close by in the barracks, received a parcel (which was almost every day) his heart ached because there wasn't one for him. And though he'd strictly forbidden his wife to send him anything even for Easter, and though he never thought of reading the list except for some rich squad member, every now and then he felt himself longing for someone to run up and say: "Shukhov! Why don't you go for your parcel? There's one for you."

But no one ran up.

He had less and less cause to remember Temgenovo and his home there. Life in camp wore him out from reveille to bedtime, with not a second for idle reflections.

Now as he stood among men who were buoying themselves up with the hope of soon digging their teeth into bits of salt pork, of spreading butter on their bread, or sweetening their mugs of tea with lumps of sugar, Shukhov had one wish only—to reach the mess hall in time and to eat his stew hot. It was only half as good when it was cold.

He figured that if Tsezar's name hadn't turned up on the list he would have gone back to the barracks long ago to wash. But if he'd found it there he would now be collecting bags, plastic mugs, and a basin. That would take him ten minutes. And Shukhov had promised to wait.

There in line Shukhov learned some news. Again there wasn't going to be a Sunday this week; again they were going

to steal one of their Sundays. He, like everyone else, had expected it, for if there happened to be five Sundays in a
month, they gave them three and made them work the other
two. Shukhov had expected it, but when he heard it a spasm
of pain caught his heart: who wouldn't begrudge the loss of
that sweet day? Though what they were saying in the line
was right: they knew how to keep them jumping even on
Sundays. They'd invent something—fixing up the baths, or
building a wall somewhere, or cleaning up the yard. There
were mattresses to be changed and shaken, bedbugs in the
bunk frames to be exterminated. Or they'd have the idea of
checking you with your photo. Or of carrying out an in-
ventory—turning you with all your things into the yard and
keeping you there half the day.

Nothing seems to make the authorities madder than zeks
napping quietly after breakfast.

The line was moving, though slowly. People were coming
in and shoving into the head of the line without even a
pardon-me, just elbowing through to the front—a camp
barber, a bookkeeper, a man who worked in the C.E.D. But
they weren't rank-and-file, they were respectable trusties,
pigs of the first order with soft jobs in the camp. The zeks
who worked outside thought them lower than —— (a rat-
ing the trusties returned). But it was futile to protest—the
trusties were a gang all their own, and were also in solid with
the guards.

Now there were only ten ahead of Shukhov. Another
seven had hurried in to line up behind him, when Tsezar,

stooping, appeared in the doorway, wearing the new fur hat that had been sent him from outside.

Now take that hat. Tsezar must have tickled someone's palm to get permission for wearing a town hat so clean and new. They even robbed others of their bedraggled service hats. Here, wear the camp pig-fur model!

A strange-looking fellow with glasses was standing in line, his head buried in a newspaper. Tsezar at once made for him.

"Aha, Pyotr Mikhailych."

They bloomed like a couple of poppies. The strange-looking fellow said: "Look what I've got! A fresh *Vechorka*.[1] They sent it by airmail."

"Really," said Tsezar, sticking his nose into the newspaper. How on earth could they make out such tiny print in the glimmer of that miserable lamp?

"There's a most fascinating review of a Zavadsky première."

Those Muscovites can smell one another at a distance, like dogs: they sniff and sniff when they meet in a way of their own. They talk so fast too, each trying to outtalk the other. When they're jabbering away like that you hear practically no Russian; they might be talking Latvian or Rumanian.

However, Tsezar had all his bags with him—everything in order.

"So I can . . . er . . . Tsezar Markovich," lisped Shukhov, "I'll take off now."

---

[1] *Vecheruyaya Moskva*—an evening newspaper.

"Of course, of course," said Tsezar, raising his dark mustache above the top of the newspaper. "Tell me though, who's in front of me? And who's behind me?"

Shukhov told him his place in the line and then, with a gentle hint, asked: "Do you want me to bring you your supper?"

(That meant from the mess hall to the barracks, in a mess tin. This was strictly against the rules—there'd been many made about it. When they caught you they poured your food out of the mess tin onto the ground and put you in the guardhouse. All the same, food was carried and would go on being carried, because if a zek has anything to do he'll never find time to go to the mess hall with his squad.)

Shukhov asked: "Do you want me to bring you your supper?" but murmured to himself: "Surely he won't be stingy. Won't he give me his supper? After all, there's no kasha for supper, only thin stew."

"No, no," said Tsezar with a smile. "Eat it yourself, Ivan Denisovich."

That was just what Shukhov was expecting. And now, like a bird on the wing, he darted from the porch and ran from one zone to the other.

The prisoners were scurrying in all directions. There was a time when the camp commandant had issued yet another order: on no account were prisoners to walk about the camp on their own. Wherever possible, a squad was to go intact. But when there could be no business for a whole squad to do at once—at the dispensary, say, or at the latrines—then groups of four or five were to be formed and a senior appointed to head them and take them there and back in a body.

The camp commandant took a very firm stand on that order. No one dared contradict him. The guards picked up solitary prisoners, took down their numbers, yanked them off to the cells—yet the order was a flop. It flopped quietly, like many much-touted orders. Someone, say, is sent for by the security boys—must you take another four or five with you? Or you have to get your food from the warehouse. Why the hell should I go with you? Someone has the strange idea of going to the C.E.D. to read newspapers. Who wants to go with him? And this fellow goes to have his boots mended, another to the drying shed, a third merely from one barracks to another (that's forbidden more strictly than anything else)—how can you hold them all back?

With that rule of his the commandant would have robbed them of their last shred of freedom, but it didn't work out, much as he tried, the fat pig.

Hurrying along the path, meeting a guard on the way and, to be on the safe side, taking off his hat to him, Shukhov ran into the barracks. The place was in an uproar: someone's bread ration had been swiped during the day and the poor fellow was shouting at the orderlies and the orderlies were shouting back. But the 104th's corner was empty.

Shukhov was always thankful if, on returning to camp, he found that his mattress hadn't been turned over and that the guards hadn't been snooping around. So that's all right.

He hurried to his bunk, taking off his coat as he ran. Up with the coat, up with the mittens and the nice bit of blade. He probed the depths of his mattress—the bread was there. Good that he'd sewn it in.

And out he ran. To the mess hall.

He reached it without meeting a guard—only a couple of zeks arguing over their bread ration.

Outside the moon shone brighter than ever. The lamps seemed to be paler now. The barracks cast deep shadows. The door to the mess hall lay beyond a broad porch with four steps. Now the porch too lay in shadow. But above it a small lamp was swaying, and creaking dismally in the cold. The light it cast was rainbow-hued, from the frost maybe, or the dirt on the glass.

The camp commandant had issued yet another strict order: the squads were to enter the mess hall in double file. To this he added: on reaching the steps they were to stay there and not climb onto the porch; they were to form up in fives and remain standing until the mess orderly gave them the go-ahead.

The post of mess orderly was firmly held by "the Limper." Because of his lameness he'd managed to get classed as disabled, but he was a hefty son-of-a-bitch. He'd got himself a birch club, and standing on the porch would hit anyone who came up the steps without his say-so. No, not anyone. He was smart, and could tell, even in the dark, when it was better to let a man alone—anyone who might give him as good as he got. He hit the down-and-outs. Once he hit Shukhov.

He was called an orderly. But, looking closer into it, he was a real prince—he palled around with the cooks.

Today all the squads may have turned up together or there may have been delay in getting things in order, but there was quite a crowd on the porch. Among them was the Limper, with his assistant. The mess chief himself was there too. They were handling the crowd without guards—the bruisers.

The mess chief was a fat pig with a head like a pumpkin and a broad pair of shoulders. He was bursting with energy and when he walked he seemed nothing but a lot of jerks, with springs for arms and legs. He wore a white lambskin hat without a number on it, finer than any civilian's. And his waistcoat was lambskin to match, with a number on it, true, but hardly bigger than a postage stamp—thanks to Volkovoi. He bore no number at all on his back. He respected no one and all the zeks were afraid of him. He held the lives of thousands in his hands. Once they'd tried to beat him up but all the cooks—a prize bunch of thugs they were—had leaped to his defense.

Shukhov would be in hot water if the 104th had already gone in. The Limper knew everyone by sight and, with his chief present, wouldn't think of letting a man in with the wrong squad; he'd make a point of putting the finger on him.

Prisoners had been known to slip in behind the Limper's back by climbing over the porch railings. Shukhov had done it too. But tonight, under the chief's very nose, that was out of the question—he'd bust you so bad that you'd only just manage to drag yourself off to the doctor.

Get along to the porch and see whether, among all those identical black coats, the 104th was still there.

He got there just as the men began shoving (what could they do? it would soon be time to turn in) as though they were storming a stronghold—the first step, the second, the third, the fourth. Got there! They poured onto the porch.

"Stop, you ——ers," the Limper shouted and raised his stick at the men in front. "Get back or I'll bash your heads in."

"What can we do about it?" they yelled back at him. "The men at the back are pushing us."

That was true, but those up in front were offering little resistance. They hoped to dash through into the mess hall.

The Limper put his club across his chest—it might have been a barricade in a street battle—and rushed headlong at the men in front. His assistant, the trusty, shared the stick with him, and so did the mess chief—who had apparently decided to soil his hands with it.

They pushed hard—they had plenty of strength, with all that meat in them. The zeks reeled back. The men in front toppled down onto the men behind them, bowled them over like wheat stalks.

"You ——ing Limper, we'll fix you," cried a man in the crowd, hiding behind the others. As for the rest, they fell without a word, they got up without a word—as quick as they could, before being stepped on.

The steps were clear. The mess chief went back to the porch but the Limper stayed on the top.

"Form fives, blockheads," he shouted. "How many times have I told you I'll let you in when I'm ready?"

Shukhov imagined that he saw Senka's head right in front of the porch. He felt wildly elated, and using his elbows made an effort to push through to him. But, looking at those backs, he knew that it was beyond his strength. He wouldn't get through.

"Twenty-seventh," the Limper called, "go ahead."

The 27th bounded up and made a dash for the door, and the rest surged after them. Shukhov, among them, was shoving with all his might. The porch quivered, and the lamp overhead protested shrilly.

"What again, you ——s?" the Limper shouted in rage. Down came his stick, on a shoulder, on a back, pushing the men off, toppling one after another.

Again he cleared the steps.

From below Shukhov saw Pavlo at the Limper's side. It was he who led the squad to the mess hall—Tiurin wouldn't lower himself by joining in the hullabaloo.

"Form fives, hundred and fourth," Pavlo called from the porch. "Make way for them, friends."

Friends—just see them making way, —— 'em.

"Let me through, you in front. That's my squad," Shukhov grunted, shoving against a back.

The man would gladly have done so but others were squeezing him from every side.

The crowd heaved, pushing away so that no one could breathe. To get its stew. Its lawful stew.

Shukhov tried something else. He grasped the porch rail on his left, got his arms around a pillar, and heaved himself up. He kicked someone's knee and caught a blow in the ribs;

a few curses, but he was through. He planted a foot on the edge of the porch floor, close to the top step, and waited. Some of his pals who were already there gave him a hand.

The mess chief walked to the door and looked back.

"Come on, Limper, send in two more squads."

"One hundred and fourth," shouted the Limper. "Where d'you think *you're* crawling, ———?"

He slammed a man from another squad on the back of the neck with his stick.

"One hundred and fourth," shouted Pavlo, leading in his men.

"Whew!" gasped Shukhov in the mess hall. And, without waiting for Pavlo's instructions, he started looking for free trays.

The mess hall seemed as usual, with clouds of steam curling in through the door and the men sitting shoulder to shoulder—like seeds in a sunflower. Others pushed their way through the tables, and others were carrying loaded trays. Shukhov had grown used to it all over the years and his sharp eyes had noticed that S 208 had only five bowls on the tray he was carrying. This meant that it was the last tray-load for his squad. Otherwise the tray would have been full.

He went up to the man and whispered in his ear: "After you with that tray."

"Someone's waiting for it at the counter. I promised. . . ."

"Let him wait, the lazy bastard."

They came to an understanding.

S 280 carried his tray to the table and unloaded the bowls.

Shukhov immediately grabbed it. At that moment the man it had been promised to ran up and tried to grab it. But he was punier than Shukhov. Shukhov shoved him off with the tray —what the hell are you pulling for?—and threw him against a post. Then putting the tray under his arm, he trotted off to the serving window.

Pavlo was standing in the line there, worried because there was no empty tray. He was delighted to see Shukhov. He pushed the man ahead of him out of the way: "Why are you standing here? Can't you see I've got a tray?"

Look, there was Gopchik—with another tray.

"They were arguing," he said with a laugh, "and I grabbed it."

Gopchik will do well. Give him another three years—he has still to grow up—and he'll become nothing less than a bread-cutter. He's fated for it.

Pavlo told him to hand over the second of the trays to Yermolayev, a hefty Siberian who was serving a ten-year stretch, like Shukhov, for being caught by the Germans; then sent him to keep an eye on any table where the men might be finishing. Shukhov put his tray down and waited.

"One hundred and fourth," announced Pavlo at the counter.

In all there were five of these counters: three for serving regular food, one for zeks on special diets (ulcer victims, and bookkeeping personnel, as a favor), and one for the return of dirty dishes (that's where the dish-lickers gathered, sparring with one another). The counters were low—about waist level. The cooks themselves were out of sight; only their hands, and the ladles, could be seen.

The cook's hands were white and well cared for, but huge and hairy: a boxer's hands, not a cook's. He took a pencil and made a note on the wall—he kept his list there.

"One hundred and fourth—twenty-four portions."

Pantaleyev slopped into the mess hall. Nothing wrong with him, the son-of-a-bitch.

The cook took an enormous ladle and stirred, stirred, stirred. The soup kettle had just been refilled, almost up to the brim, and steam poured from it. Replacing the huge ladle with a smaller one he began serving the stew in twenty-ounce portions. He didn't go deep.

"One, two, three, four. . . ."

Some of the bowls had been filled while the stuff from the bottom of the kettle hadn't yet settled after the stirring, and some were duds—nothing but soup. Shukhov made a mental note of which was which. He put ten bowls on his tray and carried them off. Gopchik waved from the second row of posts.

"Over here, Ivan Denisovich, over here."

No horsing around with bowls of stew. Shukhov was careful not to stumble. He kept his throat busy too.

"Hey you, H 920. Gently, uncle. Out of the way, my boy."

It was hard enough, in a crowd like this, to carry a single bowl without slopping it. He was carrying ten. Just the same, he put the tray down safely, on the end of the table that

Gopchik had cleared. No splashes. He managed, too, to maneuver the tray so that the two bowls with the thickest stew were just opposite the place he was about to sit down in.

Yermolayev brought another ten bowls. Gopchik ran off and came back with Pavlo, the last four in their hands.

Kilgas brought the bread tray. Tonight they were being fed in accordance with the work they had done. Some got six ounces, some nine, and Shukhov twelve. He took a piece with a crust for himself, and six ounces from the middle of the loaf for Tsezar.

Now from all over the mess hall Shukhov's squad began streaming up, to collect their supper and eat it where they could. As he handed out the bowls, there were two things he had to take care of: he had to remember whom he'd served, and he had to watch out for the tray—and for his own corner of it. (He put his spoon into a bowl—one of the "thick" ones. Reserved, that meant.) Fetiukov was among the first to arrive. But he soon walked off, figuring there was nothing to be scrounged that particular evening; better to wander around the mess, hunting for leftovers (if someone doesn't finish his stew and pushes his bowl back, there are always people hustling to pounce on it, like vultures).

Shukhov counted the portions with Pavlo. Correct, apparently. He pushed across a bowl for Tiurin, one of the "thick" ones; and Pavlo poured his stew into a narrow German mess-tin, with a lid—you could carry it under your coat, close to your chest.

The empty trays were handed in. Pavlo sat there with his

double helping, Shukhov with his two bowls. And now they had nothing more to say to one another—the sacred moments had come.

Shukhov took off his hat and laid it on his knees. He tasted one bowl, he tasted the other. Not bad—there was some fish in it. Generally, the evening stew was much thinner than at breakfast: if they're to work, prisoners must be fed in the morning; in the evening they'll go to sleep anyway.

He dug in. First he only drank the broth, drank and drank. As it went down, filling his whole body with warmth, all his guts began to flutter inside him at their meeting with that stew. Goo-ood! There it comes, that brief moment for which a zek lives.

And now Shukhov complained about nothing: neither about the length of his stretch, nor about the length of the day, nor about their swiping another Sunday. This was all he thought about now: we'll survive. We'll stick it out, God willing, till it's over.

He drained the hot soup from both bowls, and then tipped what was left in the second into the first, scraping it clean with his spoon. That set his mind at ease. Now he didn't have to think about the second and keep an eye or a hand on it.

Now that he could look freely he glanced at his neighbors' bowls. The one on his left was little more than water. The dirty snakes. The tricks they play! And on their fellow zeks.

He began to eat the cabbage with what was left of the soup. A potato had found its way into one of the bowls—Tsezar's. A medium-sized spud, frost-bitten, hard and sweetish. There wasn't much fish, just a few stray bits of bare backbone. But you must chew every bone, every fin, to suck the juice out of them, for the juice is healthy. It takes time, of course, but he was in no hurry to go anywhere. Today was a red-letter day for him: two helpings for dinner, two helpings for supper. Everything else could wait.

Except, maybe, that visit to the Lett for tobacco. None might be left in the morning.

He ate his supper without bread. A double helping *and* bread—that was going too far. The bread would do for tomorrow. The belly is a demon. It doesn't remember how well you treated it yesterday; it'll cry out for more tomorrow.

He ate up his stew without taking much interest in what was happening around him. No need for that: he wasn't on the lookout for extras, he was eating his own lawful portions. All the same, he noticed that when the fellow opposite got up a tall old man—U 81—sat down in his place. Shukhov knew he was in the 64th and had heard, while waiting in the parcels line, that the 64th had been sent to the Socialist Way of Life settlement that day instead of the 104th, and had spent the whole time without a chance of getting warm—putting up barbed wire, building their own zone.

He'd been told that this old man had spent years without number in camps and prisons, and that he hadn't benefited from a single amnesty. Whenever one ten-year stretch had run out they shoved another onto him right away.

Now Shukhov looked closely at the man. He held himself straight—the other zeks sat all hunched up—and looked as if he'd put something extra on the bench to sit on. There was nothing left to crop on his head: his hair had dropped out long since—the result of high living, no doubt. His eyes didn't dart after everything going on in the mess hall. He kept them fixed in an unseeing gaze at some spot over Shukhov's head. His worn wooden spoon dipped rhythmically into the thin stew, but instead of lowering his head to the bowl like everybody else, he raised the spoon high to his lips. He'd lost all his teeth and chewed his bread with iron gums. All life had drained out of his face but it had been left, not sickly or feeble, but hard and dark like carved stone. And by his hands, big and cracked and blackened, you could see that he'd had little opportunity of doing soft jobs. But he wasn't going to give in, oh no! *He* wasn't going to put his nine ounces on the dirty, bespattered table—he put it on a well-washed bit of rag.

However, he couldn't go on watching the old man—he had other things to do. He finished his supper, licked his spoon clean, and put it in his boot. He pulled his hat over his eyes, got up, picked up his bread and Tsezar's, and went out. Another porch led from the mess hall. Two more orderlies stood there: they had nothing to do except unhook the door, let people through, and slip the hook on again.

Shukhov came out with a full belly. He felt pleased with himself and decided that, although it was close to curfew, he'd run over to the Lett all the same. Instead of taking the bread to his barracks, he strode to Barracks 7.

The moon was high—clean and white, as if chiseled out of the sky. It was clear up there and there were some stars out —the brightest of them. But he had even less time for stargazing than for watching people in the mess hall. One thing he realized—the frost was no milder. One of the civilians had said, and this had been passed on, that it was likely to drop to −25° in the night, and as low as −40° toward morning.

From far away in the settlement he heard the drone of a tractor. From the direction of the main thoroughfare an excavator squealed shrilly. And creak, creak, went every pair of boots in which people walked or ran about the camp.

There was no wind.

He meant to buy the tobacco at the price he'd paid before —one ruble a glassful, though, outside, that amount would cost three times as much, and for some cuts even more. In forced-labor camps all prices were local; it was quite different from anywhere else, because you couldn't save money and few had any at all, for it was very hard to come by. No one was paid a kopeck for his work (at Ust-Izhma he'd received at least thirty rubles a month). If anyone's relatives sent money by mail he didn't get it in cash anyway; it was credited to his personal account. You could draw on a personal account once a month at the commissary to buy soap, moldy biscuits, and "Prima" cigarettes. Whether you liked the wares or not, you had to spend the amount the chief had given you a slip for. If you didn't, the money was lost—simply written off.

Shukhov did private jobs to get money, making slippers out of customers' rags—two rubles a pair—or patching torn jackets, price by agreement.

Barracks 7, unlike Barracks 9, wasn't in two big halves. It had a long passage, with ten doors opening off it. Each room housed a squad, packed into seven tiers of bunks. In addition, there was a little cubbyhole for the bucket and another for the senior orderly. The artists had a cubbyhole to themselves, too.

Shukhov headed for the Lett's room. He found him lying on a lower bunk, his feet propped on a ledge. He was talking to his neighbor in Latvian.

Shukhov sat down beside him. "Evening." "Evening," replied the Lett, without lowering his feet. The room was small, everyone was listening. Who was he? What did he want?

Both Shukhov and the Lett realized that people were curious, so Shukhov let the conversation drag on. Well, how are you doing? Oh, not so bad. Cold today. Yes.

Shukhov waited until everyone had started talking again. (They were arguing about the Korean war—now that the Chinese had joined in, would that mean a world war or not?) He leaned closer to the Lett.

"Any t'bacca?"

"Yes."

"Let's see it."

The Lett dropped his feet off the ledge, put them on the floor, sat up. He was a mean fellow, that Lett—filled a glass with tobacco as if he was afraid of putting in a single pinch too many.

He showed Shukhov his tobacco pouch and slid open the fastener.

Shukhov took a pinch and laid the leaf on his palm. He examined it. Same as last time, brownish, same rough cut. He held it to his nose and sniffed. That was the stuff. But to the Lett he said: "Not the same, somehow."

"The same, the same," the Lett said testily. "I never have any other kind. Always the same."

"All right," said Shukhov. "Stuff some into a glass for me. I'll have a smoke and perhaps take a second glassful."

He said "stuff" on purpose, because the Lett had the habit of dropping the tobacco in loosely.

The Lett brought out another pouch from under his pillow, fuller than the first. He took his glass out of a locker. It was really a plastic container, but Shukhov figured it held the same as an ordinary glass.

The Lett began to fray out the tobacco into the glass.

"Push it down, push it down," said Shukhov, laying his own thumb on it.

"I know how to do it," the Lett said sharply, jerking away the glass and pressing the tobacco, though lightly. He dropped in a little more.

Meanwhile, Shukhov had unbuttoned his jacket and was groping inside the cotton lining for a piece of paper that only he knew where to find. Using both hands he squeezed it along under the lining and forced it into a little hole in the cloth somewhere quite different, a small tear that he'd tacked with a couple of loose stitches. When the paper reached the hole he snapped the thread with a fingernail, folded the paper lengthwise (it had already been folded in a longish rectangle), and pulled it through the hole. Two rubles. Worn notes that didn't rustle.

In the room a prisoner shouted: "D'you mean to say you

think Old Whiskers[1] will take pity on you? Why, he wouldn't trust his own brother. You haven't a chance, you ass."

One good thing about these "special" camps—you were free to let off steam. At Ust-Izhma you need only whisper that there was a shortage of matches outside, and they'd put you in the guardhouse and add another ten years to your stretch. But here you could bawl anything you liked from the top row of bunks—the squealers didn't pass it on, the security boys had stopped caring.

The trouble was, you didn't have much time to talk in.

"Ugh, you're making it lie too loose," Shukhov complained.

"Oh well, there you are," said the Lett, adding a pinch on top.

Shukhov took his pouch out of an inside pocket and poured in the tobacco from the glass.

"All right," he said, deciding not to waste the first precious cigarette by smoking it hurriedly. "Stuff it full again."

Wrangling a bit more, he poured the second glassful into his pouch, handed over the two rubles, and left with a nod.

As soon as he was outside again he doubled back to Barracks 9. He didn't want to miss Tsezar when he came back with that package.

But Tsezar was already there, sitting on his bunk and gloating over the parcel. Its contents were laid out on his bunk and on top of the locker, but as there was no direct

[1] Stalin

light there—Shukhov's bunk was in the way—it wasn't very easy to see.

Shukhov stooped, passed between Tsezar's bunk and the captain's, and handed Tsezar his bread ration.

"Your bread, Tsezar Markovich."

He didn't say, "Well, did you get it?" That would have been to hint, "I kept that place in the line and now have a right to my share." The right was his, that he knew, but even eight years as a convict hadn't turned him into a jackal —and the longer he spent at the camp the stronger he made himself.

But his eyes were another matter. Those eyes, the hawk-like eyes of a zek, darted to one side and slid swiftly over what was laid out there; and although the food hadn't been unpacked and some of the bags were still unopened, that quick look and the evidence of his nose told him that Tsezar had got sausage, condensed milk, a plump smoked fish, salt pork, crackers, biscuits, four pounds of lump sugar and what looked like butter, as well as cigarettes and pipe tobacco—and that wasn't all.

He learned all this during the brief moment it took him to say: "Your bread, Tsezar Markovich."

Tsezar, all excited and looking a bit tipsy (and who wouldn't, after getting a parcel like that!) waved the bread away: "Keep it, Ivan Denisovich."

His bowl of stew, and now this six ounces of bread—that was a full supper, and of course Shukhov's fair share of the parcel.

And he put out of his mind any idea of getting something

tasty from what Tsezar had laid out. There's nothing worse than working your belly to no purpose.

Well, he had his twelve ounces and now this extra six, besides the piece in his mattress, at least another six ounces. Not bad. He'd eat six now and some more later, and still have next day's ration for work. Living high, eh! As for the hunk in the mattress, let it stay there! A good thing he'd found time to sew it in! Someone in the 75th had had a hunk pinched from his locker. That was a dead loss; nothing could be done about it.

People imagine that the package a man gets is a sort of nice, tight sack he has only to slit open and be happy. But if you work it out it's a matter of easy come, easy go. Shukhov had known cases when before his parcel arrived a fellow would be doing odd jobs to earn a bit of extra kasha, or cadging cigarette butts—just like anybody else. He has to share with the guard and the squad leader—and how can he help giving a little something to the trusty in the parcels office? Why, next time the fellow may mislay your parcel and a week may go by before your name appears again on the list! And that other fellow at the place where you hand in your food to be kept for you, safe from friskers and pilferers—Tsezar will be there before the morning roll call, with everything in a sack—he must have his cut too, and a good one, if you don't want him little by little swiping more than you gave him. Sitting there all day, the rat, shut up with other people's food—try to keep an eye on him! And there must be something for services like Shukhov's. And something to the bath attendant for issuing you decent underwear—not much but something. And for the barber who shaves you "with paper" (for wiping the razor on—he usually does it on your knee). Not much to him either but, still, three or four butts. And at the C.E.D., for your letters to be kept separate and not get lost. And if you want to goof off a day or two and lie in bed, instead of going to work, you have to slip the doctor something. And what about the neighbor you share a locker with (the captain, in Tsezar's case)? He must have his cut. After all, he sees every blessed ounce you take. Who'd be nervy enough not to give him his share?

So leave envy to those who always think the radish in the other fellow's hand is bigger than yours. Shukhov knows life and never opens his belly to what doesn't belong to him.

Meanwhile he pulled off his boots, climbed up to his bunk, took the strip of hacksaw out of his mitten, and decided that tomorrow he'd look around for a good pebble and start whetting down the blade to make a cobbler's knife. Four days' work, he figured, if he sat over it mornings and evenings, and he'd have a fine little knife with a sharp, curved blade.

But now he had to conceal that find of his, if only till morning. He'd slip it into the edge of the partition under the crossbeam. And as the captain hadn't returned yet to his bunk down below and the sawdust wouldn't fall on his face, Shukhov turned back the head of his mattress and set about hiding the thing.

His top-bunk neighbors could see what he was doing:

Alyosha the Baptist and—across the aisle, in the next tier—
the two Estonians. But he didn't worry about them.

Fetiukov walked through the barracks. He was sobbing,
all hunched up, his mouth smeared with blood. So he'd
been beaten up again—over the bowls! With no attempt to
hide his tears, and looking at no one, he passed the whole
squad, crawled into his bunk, and buried his face in his
mattress.

When you thought about it, you couldn't help feeling
sorry for him. He wouldn't live to see the end of his stretch.
His attitude was all wrong.

Just then the captain turned up. He looked cheerful as
he carried a pot of tea, special tea, you can bet! Two tea
barrels stood in the barracks, but what sort of tea could you
call it? Sewage: warm water with a touch of coloring, dish-
water smelling of the barrel—of steamed wood and rot. That
was tea for the workers. But the captain must have taken a
pinch of real tea from Tsezar, put it in his pot, and hurried
to the hot-water faucet. And now, well satisfied, he settled
down beside his locker.

"Nearly scalded my fingers at the faucet," he boasted.
Down there Tsezar spread a sheet of paper, and began laying this and that on it. Shukhov turned the head of his
mattress back. He didn't want to see what was going on;
he didn't want to upset himself. But even now they couldn't
get along without him; Tsezar rose to his full height, his
eyes level with Shukhov's, and winked.

"Ivan Denisovich! Er . . . lend me your 'ten days.'"

That meant a small penknife. Yes, Shukhov had one—he

kept it concealed in the partition. A bit shorter than half a finger but it cut salt pork five fingers thick. He'd made the blade himself, mounted it and whetted it sharp.

He crawled to the beam. He fished the knife out. He handed it over. Tsezar nodded and ducked below.

That knife's a breadwinner too. After all, you can be put in the cells for keeping it, and only a man without a conscience would say: lend us your knife, we're going to slice some sausage, and you can go ——— off.

Now Tsezar was again in his debt.

Having settled the bread and knife business, Shukhov opened his tobacco pouch. First he took a pinch of tobacco out of it, equal to what he'd borrowed, and stretched a hand across the aisle to Eino the Estonian. Thanks.

The Estonian's lips stretched in a sort of smile. He muttered something to his "brother," and together they rolled the pinch of tobacco into a cigarette. Let's try Shukhov's tobacco.

No worse than yours. Try it, if you please. He'd like to try it himself, but some timekeeper in his brain told him that the evening count would very soon be starting. This was just the time the guards poked around the barracks. If he was going to smoke now he'd have to go into the corridor, but up there in his bunk he somehow felt warmer. The barracks was, as a matter of fact, far from warm—that film of frost was still on the ceiling. He'd shiver in the night, but now it was bearable.

Shukhov stayed in his bunk and began crumbling little

bits off his bread. He listened unwillingly to Tsezar and Buinovsky, talking below over their tea.

"Help yourself, captain. Help yourself, don't hold back. Take some of this smoked fish. Have a slice of sausage."

"Thanks, I will."

"Spread some butter on that bread. It's real Moscow bread."

"D'you know, I simply can't believe they're still baking pure white bread anywhere. Such luxury reminds me of a time when I happened to be in Archangel...."

The two hundred voices in Shukhov's half of the barracks were making a terrific din, but he fancied he heard the rail being struck. No one else seemed to have heard it. He also noticed that "Snubnose," the guard, had come into the barracks. He was no more than a boy, small and rosy-cheeked. He was holding a sheet of paper, and it was clear from this and his manner that he'd come, not to turn them all out for the evening count or catch smokers, but to get someone.

"Snubnose" checked something on his list and said: "Where's the hundred and fourth?"

"Here," they answered. The Estonians hid their cigarettes and waved away the smoke.

"Where's the squad leader?"

"Well?" said Tiurin from his bunk, lowering his feet reluctantly.

"Your people signed those forms—about the extra stuff they were wearing?"

"They'll sign them," said Tiurin with assurance.

"They're overdue."

"My men haven't had much education. It's not an easy job. (This about Tsezar and the captain! What a squad leader! Never at a loss for an answer.) No pens. No ink."

"Ought to have them."

"They take them away from us."

"Well, look out, squad leader. If you go on talking like that I'll put you in the guardhouse with the rest," "Snub-nose" promised Tiurin, but mildly. "Now about those forms —see they're handed in to the guardroom before roll call tomorrow morning. And give orders that all prohibited garments are to be surrendered to personal property. Get that?"

"I get it."

(The captain was in luck, thought Shukhov. He hadn't heard a word, he was having such a fine time with his sausage.)

"Let's see now," said the guard. "S 311. He one of yours?"

"Have to look at my list," said Tiurin vaguely. "Expect me to keep all those damned numbers in my head?"

(He was playing for time. He wanted to save Buinovsky one night at least, by dragging things out till the count.)

"Buinovsky. He here?"

"Eh? Here I am," called the captain from his haven under Shukhov's bunk.

There you are; the quickest louse is always the first to be caught in the comb.

"You? Yes, that's right. S 311. Get ready."

"Where am I to go?"

"You know where."

The captain sighed. He grunted. Nothing more. It must have been easier for him to take out a squadron of destroyers into the dark, stormy night than to tear himself away from this friendly chat and set out for the icy cells.

"How many days?" he asked, his voice falling.

"Ten. Come on, come on. Get going."

At that moment the barrack orderlies shouted: "Evening count. All out for evening count."

This meant that the guard who was to count them had already entered the barracks.

The captain looked around. Should he take his coat? Anyway, they'd strip it off him when he got there, leaving him only his jacket. Better go as he was. He'd hoped that Volkovoi would forget (but Volkovoi never forgot anyone) and he had made no preparations, hadn't even hidden a pinch of tobacco in his jacket. And to carry it in his hands—that would be useless; they'd take it from him the minute they frisked him.

All the same . . . Tsezar slipped him a couple of cigarettes as he put on his hat.

"Well, brothers, good-by," said the captain with an embarrassed nod to his fellow prisoners, and followed the guard out.

A few voices shouted: Keep your chin up. But what could you really say to him? They knew the cells, the 104th did; they'd built them. Brick walls, cement floor, no windows, a stove they lit only to melt the ice on the walls and make pools on the floor. You slept on bare boards, and if you'd any teeth left to eat with after all the chattering they'd be doing, they gave you nine ounces of bread day after day and hot stew only on the third, sixth, and ninth.

Ten days. Ten days "hard" in the cells—if you sat them out to the end, your health would be ruined for the rest of your life. T.B. and nothing but hospital for you till you kicked the bucket.

As for those who got fifteen days "hard" and sat them out —they went straight into a hole in the cold earth.

As long as you're in the barracks—praise the Lord and sit tight.

"Come on now, out you get, before I count three," shouted the barracks commander. "Anyone who isn't out will have his number taken. I'll give it to the guard."

The barracks commander was one of the biggest bastards. After all, just think, he's locked in with us all night, but the way he acts, not afraid of anyone! On the contrary, everyone's afraid of him. Some of us he betrays to the guards, others he wallops himself. He lost a thumb in a scrap and is classed as an invalid, but his face is the face of a thug. Actually he *is* a thug with a criminal record, but among the charges against him was one under Article 58, 14, and that's how he landed in with us.

He wouldn't think twice about taking your number and passing it to the guard—and that means two days in the guardhouse, with work. So instead of just trailing to the door one by one they all rushed out in a crowd, tumbling down from the bunks as if they were bears and pressing to the narrow exit.

Shukhov, the cigarette in his palm—he'd craved it so long

and had already rolled it—sprang nimbly down, and slipped his feet into the valenki. He was on the point of leaving when he felt a twinge of pity for Tsezar. It wasn't that he wanted to make anything more out of the man; he felt genuinely sorry for him. For all his high opinion of himself, Tsezar didn't know a thing about life—after collecting his parcel he shouldn't have gloated over it; he should have taken it to the storeroom right away before the evening count. Eating's something that can wait. But now what was Tsezar going to do with all that stuff? He couldn't carry his sack with him to the count. What a horselaugh that would bring! Four hundred zeks roaring their heads off. But to leave it in the barracks no matter how briefly meant that the first to run back from the count would swipe it. (At Ust-Izhma it was even crueler: there, when we came back from work, the crooks got in first and cleaned out all our lockers.)

Shukhov saw that Tsezar realized the danger. He was bustling here and there, but too late. He was stuffing the sausage and salt pork under his jacket. That at least he could save by taking it to the count.

Pityingly, Shukhov gave him some advice: "Sit here till the last moment, Tsezar Markovich. Hide here in the shadow and stay till everyone has left. And when the guard comes by the bunks with the orderlies and pokes into everything, come out and say you're feeling bad. I'll go out first and I'll be back first. That's the way. . . ."

And he ran off.

At first he elbowed his way through the crowd mercilessly

(protecting his cigarette in his fist, however). In the corridor, which served both halves of the barracks, and near the door, the men in front were hanging back, the cagy beasts, clinging in two rows to the walls on each side, leaving just enough room for any fool who liked the cold to squeeze through. They were going to stay here; they've been out all day. Why should they freeze needlessly for another ten minutes? No fools here! You croak today but *I* mean to live till tomorrow.

At any other time Shukhov too would have clung to the wall. But now he strode to the door and even grinned.

"What are you scared of, you idiots? Never seen Siberian frost before? Come outside and warm yourselves by the wolf's sun. Give us a light, uncle."

He lit his cigarette at the door and moved out onto the porch. "Wolf's sun," that's what they'd called the moon in Shukhov's village.

The moon rode high now. As high again, and it would be at its zenith. The sky was greenish-white; the rare stars shone brilliantly. The snow gleamed white, the barrack walls gleamed white. The lamps had little effect.

There was a dense black crowd outside one of the barracks. The zeks had come out for the count. They were coming out over there too. But it wasn't the sound of voices you heard from the barracks—it was the creaking of boots on the snow.

Some prisoners were coming down the steps and lining up, opposite the barracks. Five in front, then three behind.

Shukhov joined the three. After an extra bit of bread, and with a cigarette between your lips, it wasn't so bad standing there. Good tobacco—the Lett hadn't gypped him. Strong, and smelled good.

Gradually, other prisoners trailed through the door. Two or three more lines of five were forming behind him. They came out angry now. Why were those rats jostling in the corridor? Why weren't they coming out? Why should we have to freeze for them?

No zek ever saw a clock or a watch. What use were they to him anyway? All he needs to know is: will reveille sound soon? How long to roll call? How long to dinner? To the last clanging of the rail?

The evening count, everyone said, was at nine. But it never finished at nine—they would sometimes recount two or even three times. You never got away before ten. And at five o'clock next morning they hounded you out of your bunk with the first clanging of the rail. No wonder that Moldavian had dozed off down at the shop before work was over today. Wherever a zek gets a bit of warmth into him he falls asleep on the spot. You lose so much sleep during the week that on a Sunday—provided they don't send you to work—whole barrackfuls of zeks sleep the day through.

Now they're streaming forward. At last! The barracks commander and the guard were dragging them out, kicking them in the ass. Serve 'em right, the tricky bastards.

"What?" the zeks in front shouted at the latecomers. "Pretty smart, huh? Want to lick the cream off the ——, you rats? If you'd come out earlier we'd be through now."

The whole barracks had been emptied. Four hundred men—eighty ranks of five. They lined up in a column, the ones in front strictly in fives, the others any old way.

"Get into line there, you at the back," the barracks commander shouted from the steps.

They didn't move, —— 'em.

Tsezar came out shivering, pretending he was sick. At his heels were four orderlies, two from each half of the barracks, and a prisoner who limped. They stood in front so that Shukhov was now a row farther back. Tsezar was sent to the rear of the column.

The guard came out too.

"Form fives!" he shouted to the rear of the column, furiously.

"Form fives" shouted the barracks commander even more furiously.

The men didn't budge, —— 'em.

The barracks commander rushed from the porch to the rear of the column, swearing and hitting out.

But he was careful whom he hit. Only the meek ones.

The ranks formed. He came back. He shouted:

"First. Second. Third. . . ."

As soon as they'd been counted the men broke away and rushed into the barracks. All square for today with the authorities.

All square, unless there's a recount. Those parasites were such morons, they counted worse than any herdsman. For all that he may be unable to read or write, a herdsman knows if there's a calf missing when he's driving the herd.

And these parasites had been trained—whatever good it'd done them.

The previous winter there'd been no drying sheds at all for the boots, and the zeks had had to leave their valenki in the barracks night after night. So if the count was repeated, everyone had to be driven outside again, a second, a third, a fourth time—already undressed, just as they were, wrapped in blankets. Since then a drying shed had been built; it wasn't big enough for all the boots at one time, but at least each of the squads could get the benefit of it once every two or three days. So now any recount was held inside. They merely shifted the zeks from one half of the barracks to the other, counting them as they filed through.

Shukhov wasn't the first to be back, but he kept an eye on anyone ahead of him. He ran up to Tsezar's bunk and sat on it. He took off his boots, and climbed onto the top of a tier of bunks close by the stove. He put his boots on the stove—first-comer's prerogative—then back to Tsezar's bunk. He sat there cross-legged, one eye on guard for Tsezar (they might swipe his packages from under the head of his bunk), the other for himself (they might push his boots off the stove).

"Hey," he shouted, "hey you, Red. Want to get that boot in your teeth? Put your own up but don't touch other peoples'."

The prisoners poured in like a stream.

The men in the 20th shouted: "Give us your boots."

As soon as they'd left the barracks with the boots the door was locked after them. When they ran back they shouted: "Citizen chief. Let us in."

And the guards gathered in their quarters with their boards and did the bookkeeping: had anyone escaped, or was everything in order?

Well, Shukhov needn't think about such things that evening. Here came Tsezar, diving between the tiers of bunks on his way back.

"Thank you, Ivan Denisovich."

Shukhov nodded, and shot up to his bunk like a squirrel. Now he could finish his bread, smoke a second cigarette, go to sleep.

But he'd had such a good day, he felt in such good spirits, that somehow he wasn't in the mood for sleep yet.

He must make his bed now—there wasn't much to it. Strip his mattress of the grubby blanket and lie on it (it must have been '41 when he last slept in sheets—that was at home; it even seemed odd for women to bother about sheets, all that extra laundering). Head on the pillow, stuffed with shavings of wood; feet in jacket sleeve; coat on top of blanket and—Glory be to Thee, O Lord. Another day over. Thank You I'm not spending tonight in the cells. Here it's still bearable.

He lay with his head near the window, but Alyosha, who slept next to him on the same level, across a low wooden railing, lay the opposite way, to catch the light. He was reading his Bible again.

The electric light was quite near. You could read and even sew by it.

Alyosha heard Shukhov's whispered prayer, and, turning to him: "There you are, Ivan Denisovich, your soul is begging to pray. Why don't you give it its freedom?"

Shukhov stole a look at him. Alyosha's eyes glowed like two candles.

"Well, Alyosha," he said with a sigh, "it's this way. Prayers are like those appeals of ours. Either they don't get through or they're returned with 'rejected' scrawled across 'em."

Outside the staff quarters were four sealed boxes—they were cleared by a security officer once a month. Many were the appeals that were dropped into them. The writers waited, counting the weeks: there'll be a reply in two months, in one month. . . .

But the reply doesn't come. Or if it does it's only "rejected."

"But, Ivan Denisovich, it's because you pray too rarely, and badly at that. Without really trying. That's why your prayers stay unanswered. One must never stop praying. If you have real faith you tell a mountain to move and it will move. . . ."

Shukhov grinned and rolled another cigarette. He took a light from the Estonian.

"Don't talk nonsense, Alyosha. I've never seen a mountain move. Well, to tell the truth, I've never seen a mountain at all. But you, now, you prayed in the Caucasus with all that Baptist society of yours—did you make a single mountain move?"

They were an unlucky group too. What harm did they do anyone by praying to God? Every damn one of them had been given twenty-five years. Nowadays they cut all cloth to the same measure—twenty-five years.

"Oh, we didn't pray for that, Ivan Denisovich," Alyosha said earnestly. Bible in hand, he drew nearer to Shukhov till they lay face to face. "Of all earthly and mortal things Our Lord commanded us to pray only for our daily bread. 'Give us this day our daily bread.'"

"Our ration, you mean?" asked Shukhov.

But Alyosha didn't give up. Arguing more with his eyes than his tongue, he plucked at Shukhov's sleeve, stroked his arm, and said: "Ivan Denisovich, you shouldn't pray to get parcels or for extra stew, not for that. Things that man puts a high price on are vile in the eyes of Our Lord. We must pray about things of the spirit—that the Lord Jesus should remove the scum of anger from our hearts. . . ."

"Listen to me. At our church in Polomnya we had a priest . . ."

"Don't talk to me about your priest," Alyosha said imploringly, his brow furrowed with distress.

"No, listen." Shukhov propped himself up on an elbow. "In Polomnya, our parish, there isn't a man richer than the priest. Take roofing, for instance. We charge thirty-five rubles a day to ordinary people for mending a roof, but the priest a hundred. And he forks up without a whimper. He pays alimony to three women in three different towns, and he's living with a fourth. And he keeps that bishop of his on a hook, I can tell you. Oh yes, he gives his fat hand to the bishop, all right. And he's thrown out every other priest they've sent there. Wouldn't share a thing with 'em."

"Why are you talking to me about priests? The Orthodox Church has departed from Scripture. It's because their faith is unstable that they're not in prison."

Shukhov went on calmly smoking and watching his excited companion.

"Alyosha," he said, withdrawing his arm and blowing smoke into his face. "I'm not against God, understand that. I do believe in God. But I don't believe in paradise or in hell. Why do you take us for fools and stuff us with your paradise and hell stories? That's what I don't like."

He lay back, dropping his cigarette ash with care between the bunk frame and the window, so as to singe nothing of the captain's below. He sank into his own thoughts. He didn't hear Alyosha's mumbling.

"Well," he said conclusively, "however much you pray it doesn't shorten your stretch. You'll sit it out from beginning to end anyhow."

"Oh, you mustn't pray for that either," said Alyosha, horrified. "Why do you want freedom? In freedom your last grain of faith will be choked with weeds. You should rejoice that you're in prison. Here you have time to think about your soul. As the Apostle Paul wrote: 'Why all these tears? Why are you trying to weaken my resolution? For my part I am ready not merely to be bound but even to die for the name of the Lord Jesus.'"

Shukhov gazed at the ceiling in silence. Now he didn't know either whether he wanted freedom or not. At first he'd longed for it. Every night he'd counted the days of his stretch—how many had passed, how many were coming. And then he'd grown bored with counting. And then it became clear that men like him wouldn't ever be allowed to return home, that they'd be exiled. And whether his life would be any better there than here—who could tell?

Freedom meant one thing to him—home.

But they wouldn't let him go home.

Alyosha was speaking the truth. His voice and his eyes left no doubt that he was happy in prison.

"You see, Alyosha," Shukhov explained to him, "somehow it works out all right for you: Jesus Christ wanted you to sit in prison and so you are—sitting there for His sake. But for whose sake am *I* here? Because we weren't ready for war in forty-one? For that? But was that *my* fault?"

"Seems like there's not going to be a recount," Kilgas murmured from his bunk.

"Yeah," said Shukhov. "We ought to write it up in coal inside the chimney. No second count." He yawned. "Might as well get to sleep."

And at that very moment the door bolt rattled to break the calm that now reigned in the barracks. From the corridor ran two of the prisoners who'd taken boots to the drying shed.

"Second count," they shouted.

On their heels came a guard.

"All out to the other half."

Some were already asleep. They began to grumble and move about, they put their boots on (no one ever took his wadded trousers off at night—you'd grow numb with cold unless you wore them under your blanket).

"Damn them," said Shukhov. Mildly, because he hadn't gone to sleep yet.

Tsezar raised a hand and gave him two biscuits, two lumps of sugar, and a slice of sausage.

"Thank you, Tsezar Markovich," said Shukhov, leaning over the edge of his bunk. "Come on now, hand up that sack of yours. I'll put it under my mattress." (It's not so easy to swipe things from the top bunks as you go by. Anyway, who'd look for anything in Shukhov's bunk?)

Tsezar handed up his sack and Shukhov hid it under the mattress. Then he waited a little till more men had been sent out—he wouldn't have to stand barefoot so long in the corridor. But the guard scowled at him and shouted: "Come on, you there in the corner."

Shukhov sprang lightly to the floor (his boots and foot-rags were so well placed on the stove it would be a pity to move them). Though he'd made so many slippers for others he hadn't a pair of his own. But he was used to this—and the count didn't take long.

They confiscate slippers too if they find them in daytime.

As for the squads who'd sent their boots to be dried, it wasn't so bad for them, now the recount was held indoors. Some wore slippers, some just their footrags, some went barefoot.

"Come on, come on," growled the guard.

"Do you want to be carried out, you ——s?" the barracks commander shouted.

They shoved them all into the other half of the barracks, and loiterers into the corridor. Shukhov stood against the wall near the bucket. The floor was moist underfoot. An icy draft crept in from the porch.

They had them all out now and once again the guard and the orderly did their round, looking for any who might be dozing in dark corners. There'd be trouble if they counted short. It would mean still another recount. Round they went, round they went, and came back to the door.

"One, two, three, four. . . ." Now they released you faster, for they were counting one by one. Shukhov managed to squeeze in eighteenth. He ran back to his bunk, put his foot on the support—a heave, and he was up.

All right. Feet back into the sleeve of his jacket. Blanket on top. Then the coat. And to sleep. Now they'd be letting everybody from the other half of the barracks into our half. But that's not our worry.

Tsezar returned. Shukhov lowered his sack to him.

Alyosha returned. Impractical, that's his trouble. Makes himself nice to everyone but doesn't know how to do favors that get paid back.

"Here you are, Alyosha," said Shukhov, and handed him a biscuit.

Alyosha smiled. "Thank you. But you've got nothing yourself."

"Eat it."

(We've nothing but we always find a way to make something extra.)

Now for that slice of sausage. Into the mouth. Getting

your teeth into it. Your teeth. The meaty taste. And the meaty juice, the real stuff. Down it goes, into your belly. Gone.

The rest, Shukhov decided, for the morning. Before the roll call.

And he buried his head in the thin, unwashed blanket, deaf now to the crowd of zeks from the other half as they jostled between the bunk frames, waiting to be counted.

Shukhov went to sleep fully content. He'd had many strokes of luck that day: they hadn't put him in the cells; they hadn't sent his squad to the settlement; he'd swiped a bowl of kasha at dinner; the squad leader had fixed the rates well; he'd built a wall and enjoyed doing it; he'd smuggled that bit of hacksaw blade through; he'd earned a favor from Tsezar that evening; he'd bought that tobacco. And he hadn't fallen ill. He'd got over it.

A day without a dark cloud. Almost a happy day.

There were three thousand six hundred and fifty-three days like that in his stretch. From the first clang of the rail to the last clang of the rail.

Three thousand six hundred and fifty-three days.

The three extra days were for leap years.

Library of Congress Cataloguing in Publication Data

Solzhenitsyn, Aleksandr Isaevich, 1918-
One Day in the Life of Ivan Denisovich.
(Time Reading Program)
Translation of Odin den' Ivana Denisovicha.
Originally published in 1963.
I. Title.
PG3488.04033   1981   891.73'44   80-28340
ISBN 0-8094-3553-5 (pbk.)
ISBN 0-8094-3552-7 (deluxe)